MEMORIES

TRAVEL-WORTH A REVISIT

PRASANTHI POTHINA

Made with ♥ on the Notion Press Platform
www.notionpress.com

Each time we recollect a memory, we meet the person.

For the heart never forgets...

I dedicate my writing to my parents

SAROJINI & JAYADEV

Contents

Foreword

Prasanthi Pothina, is a writer who can get connected to people's hearts easily, in her novel 'MEMORIES', succeeded in connecting our lives to her stories through almost every word or sentence. After going through the first few pages of the book, the reader can feel of sense of Déjá vu, where in you carry a feel, you or your loved ones have passed through that situation at some point of time in your life. As the title rightly says everyone has memories, both good and bad. Any human always loves to revisit those good memories, as the authoress aptly says through her tag line to the title, 'Travel worth a revisit'. This book is more of feelings than mere letters in black and white. I hope any reader shall place themselves as they travel through these wonderful memories. Which has a subtle message to the reader.

Bharathi, working as Manager – HR in Hindustan Petroleum Corporation Ltd., Visakh Refinery.

In the mundanity of everyday life and humdrum existence, hope shines through in fleeting moments like the glimmer of fireflies that leave us intoxicated with the beauty of aliveness. The whiff of fragrance from a bunch of blooming jasmine, when a chunky pup looks at you and wags its little tail, the pitch perfect note of a song or the shimmer of a breathtakingly clear night sky, these moments are gifts from the universe that make the ordinary extraordinary for those moments, and leave us alive again, Hope.

Every heart beats to a different tune but every being loves the song of hope.

This is Prasanthi's song of hope that she shares with us through these everyday stories. Listen to the song, enjoy the melody and feel the love and hope as each story leaves you feeling a little better and looking out for all that is good in the world.

Sangeetha is a voracious bookaholic, a dear friend and mentor to the author.

50% FOREWORD

The writer of this book, **Prasanthi** called me and requested to write a foreword to the book of short stories in English. I told her she called a wrong person explaining that I am not good with the language. She persisted and insisted and because of her persistence I took up this misadventure at her risk.

As I have already expressed about my knowledge of that language, I preferred to just write about the content of the stories and what are all of them about. Just stories for me not stories in English.

****

Before I can submit the message **Sri Vemuri Satyanarayana (Uncle) Garu**, *has written about the stories and me. I would like the readers to know why I insisted and persisted him. You could add hounded and harassed too. (Happy he didn't file a complaint with my nocturnal messages and calls for a foreword)*

He is a renowned TELUGU writer. *Very popular and has a huge circle of well-known celebrity names at his call and whom he can call and also address as good friends.*

I happened to know him through a cousin sister and as self-invited myself to a conversation that was enlightening.

A Facebook post of mine karam annam (Hot rice, drizzled with generous ghee, sprinkled with salt to taste and mixed with hot chili powder. A delicacy that reminded me of my school days and favorite dish. He, such a great man called me up personally to share a similar recipe with a slight variation from his wife's kitchen.
His memory that which he shared along with mine.

That's how **MEMORIES** *book started taking shape.*

So, tell me folks why should I not persist a foreword from such a noble person?

****

(Back to his words about me, a novice writer)

The observations I called and updated her with are only about the content of the stories in this book. The medium of language, English usage, expressions and other aspects in storytelling, which kept me interested.

That's why I called it a **50% foreword**. Because I can only describe that it's a good read. I was more playing a mentor to her. I am not worried much about my English in this foreword, as I have confessed about repeatedly earlier.

To you readers I can only suggest,
<u>HAPPY READING</u>

FROM
VEMURI SATYANARAYANA

The stories ...

SOMETIMES, the interesting thing about the story is how things change in a lighting speed because of another father, daughter entry into the story of a father and daughter!

ALWAYS, connects to many unfortunate incidents in recent post involving love marriages. How a love turns bitter when the girl turns wife and how a loving father reacts. A narration with emotion. *"I raised a tigress, in my family as far as my knowledge goes. She wouldn't let even a fly rest on me, neither let anyone speak back rudely."*
These words of the father in the story, perhaps should be an inspiration to many.

UNEXPECTEDADVICE, "That sister-in-law of yours is a piece!" Is how the author talks about Aparna. It caught me off balance. Wow! Most interesting thing in the story happens in a restaurant. A lovely sequence where Jhansi and Sujatha go back visiting memories and start singing a school song and few join in chorus. A lovely story felt like a scene in a movie.

I would like to go on but it would be plot reveal. So all I can write is that, the response of Aparna to the ladies may be many housewives (homemakers) who read the story can get inspired and follow Sujatha to call Aparna *" A piece of a girl!"*

UMBRELLA, liked the way a motivational speaker addressing students of an educational institute, as the medium to narrate what the writer wanted to communicate through the story.

Are you waiting for someone to protect you with an umbrella?

No, you shade yourself from harsh weather and other things carrying your own umbrella and opening it up when necessary to protect yourself.

When I read this story somewhere I remembered the words from the great *Telugupoet*, *SRI SRI Garu,* communicating in words to be self-dependent.

PRIVACY, this is a very small story discussing about the privacy of the people from each other. What are the boundaries? Can a mother not answer her son's phone?

This short story gives a lot for us to discuss and think. The relationships of people, their role in each other's lives are made part of the story.

THIS IS LOVE, one more very short story but a sweet one. You can feel the fragrance of love between a brother and sister, with Rakshabandan as back drop.

I WILL BE THERE, one caring gesture makes a lasting impact either between friends, relatives and of course couple. The writer has the knack of making a simple situation into a wonderful story.

AN ATTIRE TO REMEMBER, sexual abuse on women is an unending pandemic prevailing in the society, be it office, road even a secured place called home. How the dark deeds of a family member is suppressed in the so called 'FAMILY HONOR' is discussed in detail in this story.

OPEN YOUR EYES, is a story like an Anthology of the previous story. Discussing sexual abuse that hardly got a chance to see light. Using a YouTuber as a protagonist of this story, the narration gives a novelty arriving to a dark conventional realism.

WATCHING STORIES, this story has a man doing nothing at all at a tea stall. Sitting idle, no communication, sitting and minding his own thoughts. Watching people visit for a chai break and listening to their conversation. What is the story behind this man, is the story itself.

Preface

<u>Memories</u>

I am sure many heads would have turned when the title is mentioned. A person probably halting from sipping coffee or chai. A cookie half eaten, fingers frozen over the keyboard whether working on a laptop or mobile. A person pausing from the web series, movie or whatever they were watching as it continues to play. Yes, I proudly announce and present Memories that make you sojourn as you recall incidents however, they had been in the past, I am sure it was cherished. And when you smile it definitely must have a loved one in the thoughts who shared moments with you to believe in magic.

Memory is like a journal we keep visiting. The visits sometimes heal us, motivate us or leaves us pensive. Memories are treated as a past tense, the irony is the opposite. It's a key to door we lock up behind and when the need arises, we lookout for in the future. Could say they are our unscripted documents, which we stash away in the attic of our minds. And, that's what life is all about. A collection of memories, fading smiles and dried tears, that's a keepsake treasure box.

Life is another word that's close to my heart, besides memories. Yet! It never ceases to amaze me with its vicinity of power. Writing or journaling had been my best friend from the time I discovered it. How did it start, my mania for the ink, well it's a story we can talk about another day!

Hello, hai ...adab namaste this is Prasanthi Pothina and I am your narrator for this amazing book named "Memories". That's right folks.

Before I tread back to the stories let me walk a bit along with you and add a tiny version about why I chose this title.

Let me take you into a series of stories later as when the pages turn, that have captured me and taught me positivity.

Watching people, and their simple musings have helped me churn out beautiful stories. A chanced walk with different people, and lessons learnt from them made me what I am today, a small-time writer. And every time I pick up a pen to jot down a simple tale, its actually a recall of a certain incident that threaded the thought. A term coined as MEMORY.

Memory has no sensation to a touch, yet the irony is it can be felt. *Felt so deep that it touches one's heart and soul. It develops feelings though it lives in a past tense and then tends to master over us as we give it a recall. Many a time it also makes us slaves when we deny a place for it in our mind. Because we constantly remind ourselves not to think about it and in that process, we enslave ourselves to it by chain, giving it a permanent place but in denial.*

Often, I find people thinking about their past and sometimes they try to force the memories away returning to their current delusion. That's when love in the memories steps in closing the distance even as life keeps it apart, and makes one do the irrational. It makes one do the impossible, even inexcusable things out of imagination. Why does one only focus more on the pain suffered, pride hurt, a guilt shared, betrayal and think of embarrassment. Why focus on darkest memories that should be buried. Why not the ones that plant a smile on your face, whilst watching a rain, hearing a lost tune, watching a child play, a certain sentence, gesture, taste, smell. Many times, people want to drive back to their past and stay cozy for a while to rejuvenate, because there is more to the world of memories than that. That's why memories are called miracles.

Maybe I am writing this book observing people, but I can call it my original creation I guess, hmm then again, I wonder?

Stories are always cherished and here in this book let us walk into a few different concept themes. This time the stories that are narrated here are about memories that are special moments laced into a story for you. Memory opens up portals to something we cannot go back to change, but value it for it did make a big change in life we further proceeded into. Perhaps I would like to start fresh with a story that's similar to mine, and maybe a conversation that you never wanted to disclose that was similar to yours.

Acknowledgements

To my family and friends, who never grew tired with my doubts and absurd questions. Repeated questioning whether I really can pen sensible lines. Countless discussions trying to encourage me out of my procrastination.

• • •

Well, here I am with another book, if its good appreciate me, if you find anything, just anything out of place its them not me! They forced me to write.

• • •

<u>Disclaimer</u>: The stories written in this book, MEMORIES are imaginative triggers I happen to suddenly brainstorm when I was probably listening to music, drinking coffee, walking on my terrace, playing with my pets or staring blankly at the sky. Let me tell you that they are not based around any incident or people directly or indirectly.

Credits

Author: Prasanthi Pothina

Cover design by: Satish Kumar Pothina

Prologue

NEVER HURTS TO REMEMBER, talks about small things that ensures a smile on your face. A ribbon on the braid, a handkerchief pinned to the uniform when in kindergarten. A bicycle race...much more. Plain remembrance is what the story offers and nothing else.

SOMETIMES, a choice put forward may seem absurd. But when it is analyzed why? The person who presented the question will find the answer within themselves.

ALWAYS, blaming the party that has committed the mistake is not correct, the reason for it to happen maybe because ...of authoritative behavior. I told you not to do it, now face the consequences. What if the judging part was delivered in a soft manner and guide one out of the situation. The outcome will definitely be different.

THEUNEXPECTEDADVICE, can come from the least expected person who we sometimes dismiss as immature.

UMBRELLA doesn't shelter one from heat and cold but also stay like a shadow. A shield that coaxes a person to walk ahead bravely and do what they believe in.

PRIVACY, a word the youth generate and use constantly not giving it an ounce of thought that sometimes when a ball bounces on the wall one too many times, it tends to cracks it.

IWILLBE THERE; a couple don't need to proclaim love and announce it often to each other. Being supportive matters and spells more colorful than a sentence of declaration.

THIS ISLOVE, talks about what gifting really is and not materialistic things.

AN ATTIRETO REMEMBER, does a certain dressing cause abuse? Does one need to look into the mirror and judge the quality of their choice for the society to label them if they voice out an abuse?

OPEN YOUR EYES, a taboo topic, when the family doesn't give an ear or a chance to talk out. Understanding the fear in the child's eye. Sitting down and talking can help the nightmares to dismiss.

WATCHING STORIES is how stories come into existence. A break from the everyday underlined media pressure and walk into a pleasant moment can relief a person ...

CHAPTER I

Never Hurts To Remember

Bhargav watched as his colleagues unpacked their belongings, the team were churning out their classroom days, he sighed and smiled looking at the ceiling. They were at present in a school classroom prepping up to deliver their conceptual idea and let them follow the thread of lost thought at one point which felt important. The fan that was attempting to save them from the summer heat, was trying its best with a rattling sound that notified its age. He mentally made a note to himself.

'Everyone tries their best to do their part, even as their strength diminishes. The zeal to help which is a default, continues till no matter what.'

He chuckled to himself appreciating himself silently for coming up with a quote he felt was brilliant.

"Share that piece of thought running a marathon in your mind Mr. Ideas." Chandana his partner in crime placed her hand comfortably on his shoulder and stood beside him.

"At first, I wondered what's this crazy guy up too, anyways he's the boss let me play safe by showing up. But gradually I am looking forward to read the thoughts and feel nostalgic." Chandana said fidgeting with her phone camera.

Bhargav looked at his childhood friend and now his partner in business. He recollected her face at the time when he proposed his idea.

Her words at that time, *"What's the take away?"*

"Nothing." He replied to her.

She made an awry face and mimicked him, *"Nothing....?"*

"But, see everyone starts something for a reason, right? So, the same implies to your idea. I mean like your offering services for free and even the material is coming out from your pockets..." she stared at him, and he knew her thought process. She definitely must be thinking

'Dude are you thinking straight.'

"Yes, gal I am thinking straight and the whole purpose for starting this is has nothing to do with monitory gains. I kind of don't want people to lose themselves becoming a routine mechanical self. That's all."

"Whatever..." she said shrugging her shoulders.

"Yep whatever..." he said picking up his chai glass and clinking it withhers, "Cheers chandu, so I guess I can take that you're in, right?"

"I have to be, I don't want you to sail alone and drown somewhere idiot." She said with sarcasm and clinked her glass with his responding to the cheers.

"Okie's selfie time...guys join us." She said aloud cutting short Bhargav's flashback. The team gathered as she clicked multiple snaps.

"Another day, to capture the lost wishes and make the mechanical faces smile guys...let's do it." She announced. And the team felt her enthusiasm seep into them, giving them a warm glow of sunshine exhilaration.

That's when Nawaz walked up to them with a big glass bowl, "Which class am I assigned to sir?" he asked him with a newcomer's enthusiasm. It was his second day volunteering for WISHINGSTARS team.

Bhargav replied, "Today it's the assembly Nawaz."

Nawaz looked at him with warm smile. "About yesterday sir..."

Bhargav received a call just then, "Could you give me a minute? I need to take this call it's from my amma."

Nawaz waited, Bhargav walked a little further away from Chandana and Nawaz. Both looked at each other smiling uncomfortably and acknowledging the other's presence.

Chandana decided to break the silence, "So how do you feel working with WISHINGSTARS group?"

"Good ma'am." Nawaz replied promptly. He was about to add more of it when Bhargav finished his conversation and returned to hear Nawaz reply.

"Cut the formality, Nawaz. Speak your mind. Like you did yesterday with Archana." Bhargav said to him as he pocketed his mobile.

Nawaz hesitated a bit, Chandana knit her brows wondering what she had missed. She looked at Bhargav and raised her eyebrows in question of what was that line for.

"Well sir..." he dragged the sir bit.

"Go on...so did you enjoy a walk with your father and also manage to sneak in a Faluda. I guess you didn't tell your mother because of your father's diabetic condition." Bhargav made a statement to him. It caught Nawaz off guard. *"Some cheats are absolutely okay."* Bhargav said tapping Nawaz's shoulder.

"Yes, how the hell...pardon my language but were you following me or what sir?" Nawaz looked at Bhargav with astonished eyes.

Chandana hit Bhargav on his shin with her sneaker. *"Ouch fatso what was that for."* Bhargav exclaimed in pain. *"Because I am unable to follow your conversation."* She said in playful manner.

He tried to hit her on the head which she dodged and stuck her tongue out. *"There is no rule I have to tell you everything..."*

Nawaz looked at them both, waiting patiently for his question to be answered.

That's when a teacher interrupted them, walking into the classroom allotted to the team *WISHINGSTARS*. She informed them that the assembly would be starting in a minute or so, and the principal was asking for their presence.

The walked back along with the teacher to the assembly ground.

Chandana let her hand run across the school wall, humming a school song she recollected while peeped into the classrooms with a faraway look in her eyes.

Suddenly she stopped humming and blurted out, *"Present teacher."* The teacher accompanying them turned back and said, "The best part of the growing years was attendance right." Chandana agreed with a giggle.

Bhargav felt a cloud of happiness descend upon him.

He looked at Nawaz and winked. Nawaz felt out of sync.

At the assembly session *Bhargav* saw, his team singing along with the school choir and even recite the prayer. The group of seven members whispered when the, 'Thought for the day' was being presented.

"A rolling stone gathers no moss."

"Hey remember this one, silence is golden."

"My favorite was an idle brain is a devil's workshop."

"Our class teacher always reminded us of this and also I know another one, every cloud has a silver lining."

"Guys, guys how can we miss out this famous one, an apple a day keeps the doctor away."

The team was enjoying their day off with socializing yet working with his small startup idea which he had named, *WISHINGSTARS.* it had been a year since it was initialized and Bhargav was satisfied with the slow increase of invites he was receiving from corporate companies and educational institutes.

The principal delivered the message of the day, including talking about the recent activities of misbehavior by students. The importance of education. How to maintain a proper routine which will help them in the future. Bhargav watched the student's expressions. He saw their interested faces with wide eyes and knew they must be waiting for the marching tune or disperse word to relieve them from the everyday ritual. A few were eyeing who these strangers were? Some students were rubbing their black shoes on their socks to make it shine. A few standing in the back were passing something. Some whispered, winked, yawned, and as expected the call arrived, *"Teacher shaan fainted."*

The PT (Physical training) teacher ran towards the fainter, analyzed the situation and called for two students to help the boy to the infirmary.

"Ah those days..." Bhargav said to himself. The assembly always ended with at least one fainter.

He then heard his name called out, *"Let me allow Mr. Bhargav here, who is the CEO of a wonderful happiness sharing group named WISHINGSTARS. I will let him do the talking and explain. When he approached me with the idea I was thrilled and he asked permission to do the same talking to you'll. I experienced a joy which I felt should be shared with all of you students. So, students please put your hands together and welcome Mr. Bhargav."*

The response from the students was an obedient clap sound. *Bhargav* chuckled and walked towards the podium and looked at the bored faces.

He cleared his throat, *"Good morning ..."* he stopped for a few seconds and turned towards the teachers, *"Goooood Morrrrning teacherrrrss."* He said like a student. Then he further added, *"Teacher urgent..."* and put out his little finger, asking to b e excused.

The assembly ground with students roared with laughter and a few clapped. Someone even whistled.

Bhargav knew he caught the student's tempo, *"There you are in the right mind to listen. I am a very practical person and also one who keeps his eyes glued to the clock. Time is precious to beat around the bush explaining why I stand here Infront of you. so, let me be crisp and clear, I am here to catch up on your lost memories. That you've shelved and hardly have time to refresh in these hectic growing years."*

He turned towards *Nawaz,* *"Nawaz."* He called out to him.

Promptly *Nawaz* walked up to him with a bowl filled with paper strips.

Without any introduction of what's going on and why *Bhargav* was there to talk to them, *Bhargav* started reading from the strips handed over by *Nawaz.*

"My brother braiding my hair."

He noticed the children's puzzled expression including the teachers who stood behind him, he didn't stop to explain what it meant but continued.

"Grandfather teaching me how to ride a bicycle.

Grandma's sweets when she comes visiting.

Daddy coming home early and watching a film with us."

By now a few faces understood what was going on, they whispered what *Bhargav* was trying to imply. The chain of passing the message went about. *Bhargav* who was noticing it, felt the satisfaction of his task being accomplished. He didn't stop even now and went around announcing a few more sentences.

"Amma making Gulab jamun for my birthday.

My friend helping me with math's."

Chandana stepped and she continued to read from the strips, Bhargav took a step backwards and allowed her.

"When a friend shared an umbrella.

Village visits.

An uncle giving me lift to reach school on time."

A few members of his team and teachers joined Chandana and started reading along with her. Bhargav could notice the tears building up in their eyes.

"Teacher adding that extra mark that made me pass.

Got a puppy as gift.

Playing cricket with my friends.

Making paper boats during rainy season.

Playing four cups game.

Rockets making.

Drama classes."

Bhargav gestured to stop reading and watched the expression of the students.

"These are the small lines shared by corporate working people who missed and still cherish in their busy schedule. I am not here asking you to invest, buy or promote me. I shall but leave an empty bowl in each class room with paper strips. Don't need to add names or explain in length. Write if you're interested about an experience that you cherish. I will take the filled bowl to read them out to another set of strangers and place the same request. Well, that's all folks from my side."

He turned and was about to leave when he received genuine applause and shouts from the students.

"Mine is spiderman show."

"He-man and the masters of the universe."

"Kabaddi matches."

"My friends stood by me when I met with an accident."

Bhargav nodded his head, turned towards the mic and announced, "Save them to be written." He pointed at the glass bowl. He noticed the excited faces of the students discuss and understood the adrenaline rush.

A hesitant teacher approached them, *"If you could place one in our staff room too?"*

"Of course, it was already a part of our plan." He told them. A few teachers huddled and reminisced their delights wondering what to express.

Once the work was competed and the team was driving back, *Bhargav* looked at *Nawaz.*

"Yesterday when you asked Archana what work does WISHINGSTARS actually do or promote, and she briefed you about it. I heard you talk about your father who met with an accident and moves around in a wheelchair. In your questionnaire the answer to our question, what is your favorite pastime? You had written evening walks with dad and relishing faluda."

Nawaz understood what *WISHINGSTARS* agenda actually was. Connecting people back to the ones they had kept aside due to workload or other goals in life.

Bhargav who runs a software development company, had come up with this idea of volunteering along with his team once every three months visiting offices, colleges, schools, universities even hospitals. Giving back people what they had saved in memories a visit again.

What was the take away, SHARING HAPPINESS, WITH RECOLLECTION!

Gathering thoughts

When a smile breaks, informing the agenda's,

"Guys can you wait?"

Let me enjoy a moment,

Let me relish time instead of brooding and make a new friend.

Let me allow enthusiasm flow through,

A moment is what makes a huge difference in life...

And, tells us its beautiful!

CHAPTER II

Sometimes

The situation was complicated; *Divya* was standing tensed draped in a beautiful orange tissue saree with a green border that had a gold thread work design of palanquin bearers carrying a bride. She wore antique jewelry to match her attire. *Divya* was decently tall; her designer wear stilettoes made her look a tad bit taller could say. And coming to her hair it was done into a bun which had roses adorning around it, makeup was minimal, there was no need for it, *Divya* had captivating looks, a natural beauty the girl was. Ooh la la, how could we forget her well maintained hour glass figure that had heads turn wherever she went.

Right now, *Divya* was tensed for the absurd and spontaneous request she had placed Infront of her father. It actually not only caught him by surprise but her too.

Divya stood facing her father with a question in her eyes, will he or wont he. Hmm, tough decision, I guess. He swirled his wine glass as the ice clinked grabbing attention in the silent room.

"So, you want to?" that was the question asked by him to his daughter.

When she uttered the words, for a second she could sense her mind questioning herself, *"Whatttt the hell...are you serious? From where did you muster the courage to ask for such a thing? Come one Divya snap out of it, you're joking right? seriously are you nuts?"*

She attacked herself when her mind started questioning her, to which she gave her mind a block and allowed her heart to take control of the situation.

"Do I look insane babe, do I? no nah so J.U.S.T back off. Over and out." That was the threat which let her reasoning mind understand nothing is going to make her break her decision.

Where was the story exactly? yeah and she, that is *Divya* was looking with pleading eyes at him that's her father right now. The two of them had excused themselves from the Banquet Hall previously and retired to the guest room.

The ice clinked against the glass in a rough manner, it showed the anger that *Divya's* father masked with a calm posture as he swirled it in deep thought.

She was expecting him to give her a lecture and then threat or whatever the fathers in Indian cinema's do when their daughters refuse to marry the chosen person.

Her father was deep in thought.

Divya was waiting for her father to say something to her. Why was Divya tensedand scared while waiting for her father to say something to her?

Because, it was *Divya's* engagement and when she was dressing up rather dolling up herself, she remembered the dinner date with her aunty, her mother's sister at the **Caribbean night's restaurant.** *The seafood there is amazing and the coconut cocktail is a must try I recommend it personally. The Oyster shells well done Soft, plump and juicy oven baked with a garlic and curry leaf butter emulsion, coriander leaves and Kashmiri chilli powder. A taste that melts into your mouth.*

Okay fine I did it again diverting myself from what the story is actually.

So, her aunt said to her, *"Happy for you Divya to see you stepping into a marital world."*

Divya smiled and went ahead sipping her cocktail. Her fork ran randomly over the Russian salad.

Her aunt put down her wine glass and shook her head. *"Are you in love with him?"* she asked her slowly.

A waiter was seen walking up to them, her aunt sent him away without a word spoken but a look that read, *"Don't disturb us."* He nodded his head in acknowledgement and turned his attention to another table.

"He is kind, nice and listens to me patiently." Divya said as a matter of fact.

"Okay...but are you in love with him?"

"Well, he got me presents, we watched a film. He knew what popcorn I like and then we lunched twice, I guess. He knew my preferences and bought me flowers and other expensive gifts." Divya went on like a parrot and her aunt listened to her uncomplainingly.

"Okay darling lets finish our dinner." She said to *Divya* with a smile.

"I guess that's love." Divya almost whispered to her aunt in a tone that was laced with a doubt.

Divya looked at her aunt, who had no intention of resuming the previous question.

She looked at the presents her aunt had given her which were placed precariously on the seat next to her, with a bouquet adjacent to it. He eyes rolled over the items spread on the table that were smiling back at her as if in conversation, *"Hi Divya we meet again."* the regularized menu spread was what she saw.

Everything was fitting like a jigsaw puzzle, in a frame that was provided. It was arranged to make her feel at home. This was love for sure, her aunt knew what she preferred.

But was this what she preferred?

What if she encountered something different and wanted to try it?

Will it not excite her and add on to her list?

A step out of the comfort zone of providence. She was given what she asked for after monitoring. She was told what she had to have and she felt satisfied.

She let her glance fall on her aunt, who was now on a call, the question she asked her, "Are you in love with him.?" *What did she mean exactly?*

She spent time with him and felt he was understanding and ...

Divya's thoughts were breached. *It was a choice taken and presented to her, was it not?*

Her father's voice got her back to reality.

"I asked your consent before I could arrange for this engagement, right?" his voice was rough and sounded stern.

She nodded her head.

"But..." her explanation was cut off.

"I also showed you his photograph and gave you time to decide?" he told her which sounded more like an interrogation that she was given a statement prior and it was now being recalled to let her know that she was asked and that it was not a compulsion.

She nodded her head again in affirmation.

"I think I need more than a head nod Divya." He said raising his voice. *"I've got people out there to explain."* She could feel the heat increasing in his tone.

"Do you think what you asked for is right?"

She shuddered. The storm was brewing she knew.

"More than thinking if its right, how could you even think of placing such a request?"

A few seconds of silence passed between them which gradually inched towards minutes.

She tried to answer him, but she choked on her words. that's when there was a knock on the door and the doorknob turned.

Her eyes widened as he stepped in, *A towering personality who sported a peppered wavy hair. He was brown skinned, a round face which held sharpness, his eyes were dark brown. A dark blue Chinese collared Lenin shirt was clutching his lean yet muscular body as if stitched on to him. The shirt complimented his beige regular fit cotton trousers. The black loafers on his feet, seemed to make him glide into the room rather than step in.*

"Excuse me sir if you could give me a minute of your time, I would like to untie the knots the present scenario is in." he said.

His hand was clasping a little one who was hiding behind him, she in turn was clasping a cuddle with frightened eyes. *Divya's* heart melted.

"And you are?"

"Vijay Amarnath sir, Amarnath group of companies CEO." He offered an extended hand to her father, which was contemplated at first and then a firm handshake followed.

He pulled up a seater for *Divya* and asked her to sit down, *"Please."* He said to her.

After which he sat down comfortably with his child preaching on his lap. Her curls covered her face. she seemed aware of her surroundings, and that the air was filled with discomfort that made her feel uneasy.

"With your permission sir, I would like to talk to her." He rather stated than asked. It reminded *Divya* of her father, who took control of situations.

Divya glanced at her father if he would give permission to a stranger? she was surprised to see him raise his hand as if in acknowledgment.

"Be my guest." He added.

Divya looked sideways narrowing her eyes and threw up her hands, *"Whattt.... I cannot believe it...woah hold a minute..."* which was cut off by *Vijay,* who now faced her and opened his dialogue.

The voice, his voice it was commanding yet, held a smooth deep confidence to it and instead of enhancing the awkwardness of the situation it relaxed her.

"So, Divya, it's Divya, right?" he didn't wait for her to say yes but continued with his dialogue.

"Coming to the fact we've never met before anddd." He stressed on the and bit before resuming what he wanted to tell her.

"Okay right and this is the first time we are seeing each other, of course we can dismiss the incident of you finding my daughter Pranavi in the parking lot and all that a few hours ago." he said to her off handedly.

Divya shook her head in agreement.

"We did meet right recently in the reception after the announcement was made? You waited along with her and then took her to the stationary." He pulled out a book from *Pranavi's* bag and showed it to her.

"This coloring book you bought her, the crayons with which both of you drew pictures to make a greeting card and from there the visit to the toy shop, you got her this panda bag too right." he looked about and he saw his daughter was clutching on to it dearly. He pointed to the bag.

"That one."

Divya shook her head again biting her lips. Her eyes were welling up. Her father was about to say something to *Vijay* when,

"That's okay I know your tensed and all. I won't deny that there is an unpleasant spot between us. Due to which, you are all confused. I get it. It's okay. Relax no one is blaming you. if your father is sitting here and giving you time to explain and waiting it's because he loves you. He wants the best of you. okay."

Divya's father sniffled hearing *Vijay* talking to his daughter and reached for his glass to sip and then noticed *Pranavi* looking at him with large eyes. he softened a bit; she reminded him of *Divya*.

"I am sorry can I offer you something?" he asked *Vijay*.

"No thank you." was all *Vijay* said to him, he now saw *Divya* seemed to feel better and resumed his conversation.

"Okay fine that's clear then ...why did you bother to help Pranavi? Is it because she looked like a well-dressed kid and was found in a posh resort parking lot?" the question threw both Divya and father off balance.

"Gosh no, what the hell man?" *Divya* said to him angrily.

Vijay relaxed, placing *Pranavi* comfortably on his lap.

He caught a nerve and now he knew she was going to come out with her thoughts which were all scooped up and hidden in an attic inside her brain.

"How could you even say that? I was not interested in going ahead with the engagement. I walked out of the resort to leave without anyone's knowledge. What Saritha aunty said was true. I needed to find a person who loved me, not my position or or ..." she was racking her brain for the proper words.

"Father's bank balance." Both *Vijay* and *Divya's* father chorused together. They looked at each other and smiled.

"Yeah that, so I couldn't get to tell my father who might not want me to back off in the last minute and I was leaving the premises quietly. I saw Pranavi earlier I mean last night when you guys wait a minute ...no that was in the evening yes, in the evening the way you spent time with her and made her feel comfortable."

She screwed up her face and was racking her brains to point out places where she saw them and also hand over a possible explanation.

"It reminded me of dad. That's why I started following you guys, toy shop, when you took her out for a cycle ride, near the beach remember you made a fairy in the sand sprawling on all four. gosh, that was something I was sooo. Hmm I donno. Who in the right sense of mind would get his suit spoilt in the beach sand? You hardly even noticed it. Then you two enjoyed a spicy corn, done on the charcoal. That's one of my favorites too. You read her a book later on while she enjoyed on the swing. It made me cry. Not a sad cry, cry like in happiness."

Divya stopped for a minute. *"Okay that was all about yesterday and about why I was with Pranavi was..."* her eyes brightened and she garnered courage and faced him with confidence.

"And then when I was leaving this evening, I saw her helpless in the parking lot, I was concerned for her and you. she was scared. I imagined you, how much tension you must be taking that she was missing. I knew thoughts might be running like kidnap or accident something." *Divya* said raising her hands in the air animatedly.

"I didn't want you to miss her, the way you looked after her I knew her mother was not around, I mean alive in this world. That's why I came back and reported in the front desk and made them announce. I didn't want to leave her in someone's care. No, it was not right. She was frightened. After she felt comfortable with me, she came out with a reason why she walked out of the room unattended. It was to buy stationary to make a card for you. it's your birthday today right. She wanted to show her love with a greeting card drawn by her. I realized that she strayed. Since I didn't know your name, the announcement was made in her name."

Divya looked into his eyes, *"I felt a pain when she let go of my hand as soon as she saw you and ran. I was feeling selfish, because she clung to me for more an hour sobbing and calling me amma, amma."*

Divya stopped her narration and looked at her father. *"Why would I rescue a kid because they are rich or something dad, I am your child. You taught me to be kind. When I saw these two together dad.*

I remembered how much you cared for me. I meant the world to you. You sacrificed everything to bring me up. And this engagement was arranged to a person whom you would've screened a million times. But daddy I want to marry someone like you, caring and affectionate. I saw that in..." she stopped herself and faced her father.

"*I know I should've told you earlier daddy about my decision, but then I was not in love. They say love is something unexplainable, it comes on its own terms in the...*" she sniffled and looked around for a tissue.

Vijay handed her his handkerchief which she accepted without hesitation and blew into it. "*I will get it washed and return it.*" she said to him.

He gave her a smile, "*It's okay you can keep it.*"

Pranavi got down from his lap and walked up to her, "*Are you okay amma?*" She asked her placing her hand on *Divya's* lap.

Divya took *Pranavi's* hand into hers and said to her father, "*Love comes unannounced in the weirdest way. And see how it touched me now dad.*"

Vijay got up from his seat and addressed *Divya's* father.

"*So, that's what it's all about, I think I should be get going.*" *Vijay* now looked at *Pranavi* and smiled, "*Shall we ...*" he said to his daughter.

"*Just a minute Amarnath.*" *Divya's* father said to him.

Vijay stopped in his tracks, *Divya* was relieved that he stopped, for she felt her heart beat slow down when he announced he was going to take leave of them.

"*Is there anything else to talk between us?*" *Vijay* questioned him.

Divya's father smiled sarcastically.

"*Don't you think there is?*" he threw the ball into his court.

"*I am done with my explanation.*" *Vijay* said as if concluding his speech. "*I think I need to be excused as I am not a part of this anymore.*"

"*Then why?*" *Divya's* father asked him.

"*I am sorry, come again. what do you mean by why?*" this time it was *Vijay's* turn to be confused.

Divya's father smiled, he took a deep breath and exhaled. He gestured towards the chair *Vijay* was sitting previously. *Vijay* took the hint and sat down again. *Pranavi* went towards *Divya*, who welcomed her with a huge hug.

Before *Divya's* father could speak, they were interrupted with room service. it was for *Pranavi*.

"I hope you like what grandpa ordered little princess?"

Pranavi hesitated first and looked at her father, who told her it was okay she can. The little one was still musing when *Divya* took the tray and walked her into the other room.

"Let grandpa and papa talk we can enjoy these to ourselves." Vijay was touched by the look on *Pranavi's* face.

Divya's father pulled out a cigar from his case and searched for a lighter. *Vijay* lit it up for him, with his.

"I don't smoke when Divya's around." *Vijay* nodded his head in agreement.

"Me too, trying to stop the habit but some memories..." he let his sentence slide.

"Would you like to..." *Divya's* father asked him.

"No, Pranavi might walk in and I don't want her to catch me." *Vijay* said with concern.

"So, my question to you is why did you come back?" Divya's father asked him cutting back to the original script of the situation in the room.

Vijay looked at him, but his thoughts were far away. When he parked his car and the luggage was being transferred to his room, he collided with the banner guys who were putting up *Divya's* engagement banner. Coincidentally that was when *Vijay* was on call with his mother who was pestering him to marry again.

"Amma, think of Pranavi, I cannot be self-centered and marry someone. Do you think the person who will come can take Madhavi's place? show real mother's care to Pranavi like her own daughter? Be sensible amma, matches are coming because I am well settled. If not, who would want to marry a guy who has a 4-year-old kiddo?"

"You always shut me up with your reasons Vijay, world is not filled with Cinderella's stepmother's okay. I am sure there must be someone who is as understanding as you and will love you for who you are and not run after a bank balance. She will look after Pranavi as her own child. You need to open up for such a person." Vijay's mother sounded dejected as she spoke those words to him. She was sick of trying to convince her son to remarry after her daughter in laws death during childbirth. Watching her son single was breaking her heart. No amount of coaxing was making him think about marriage.

Vijay could hear her sigh and say, *"Only a miracle can change your mind and I sincerely pray for it to happen soon."* and the call got disconnected.

That's when *Divya's* banner fell on him accidentally and *Vijay* was smitten by her looks. He noticed her during the time he spent with *Pranavi* and felt a connection. He tried to look the other way, but fate seemed to be bringing them together and he saw her everywhere. He was tensed after *Pranavi* walked out on him when he was on a business conference call, and searched frantically for her in the resort.

He was relieved to hear the announcement of a four-year-old girl named *Pranavi* looking out for her father. The parent was asked to report near the front desk. He ran frantically. On seeing *Pranavi* safe clasping Divya's hand. He took large steps towards them and hugged *Divya*.

He hugged her so tight, as if he wanted to merge her into him. Suddenly, he parted from her and still catching *Divya's* hand unconsciously he knelt down and scolded *Pranavi*, *"Don't you ever leave me like that, you gave me a heart attack. I cannot be without you."*

He cried like a baby, and hugged his daughter with his left arm. His right hand was still clasping *Divya's* tightly. He was afraid to let it go. After a few minutes. He stood up, wiped his tears and faced *Divya*.

They didn't talk, nor exchange words of thank you or anything. They stood opposite and their hands still in a tight clasp. Afraid if they wake into the reality, they would've to let go of each other.

Divya's cousin found them and called out to her. they reluctantly let go. *Vijay* took hold of his daughter's hand and walked out; he was hardly earshot when he heard *Divya* asking someone who he was.

"What's Pranavi's fathers name." she asked. The front desk said something inaudible and he heard her shouting irritably, *"That guy with the girl whose name is Pranavi. You announced it nah. Her father's name."* he slowed down his pace.

He also heard her cousin scolding her why she wanted to know. *"Why do you want to know his name, the nerve of him not to even appreciate you rescuing his daughter. At least a simple thank you would've been nice."*

"I want his name because I have decided to become Pranavi's mom." She announced.

"Shut up girl, are you in your senses? Did you drink too much?" her cousin gasped, hearing *Divya.* *"Let's go Divya your father is worried about you, and have you any idea you left your engagement event and a guy waiting who has no clue of what's going on?"* Footsteps were heard coming towards *Divya.*

"Let's go now Divya you seriously have a lot of explanation to do. See the security also has arrived. I still cannot understand how you evaded these guys and walked out." Her cousin said to her.

Vijay heard Divya's cousin lecture the security about not keeping proper vigilance and how easily Divya could slip away from them.

Vijay who was shocked hearing *Divya* took time to digest her words. By the time he could react, and turn around. She had left.

For a minute he wondered if what she said was real, or was his ears playing up on him.

Vijay looked at *Divya's* father in silence as he recalled the incidents that passed between *Divya* and him.

"I came back to explain because..."

Divya's father raised his hand and stopped him from further conversation. He stood up, extinguished his cigar in the ashtray and adjusted his suit. On cue even *Vijay* stood up, still contemplating what to tell him.

"Divya..." Her father called out to her. she walked in with *Pranavi* in her arms.

The little one had a lollipop stuck in her mouth which gave her lips a red tinge.

"Hey little princess, come here." Saying *Divya's* father took her in his arms.

Both *Divya* and *Vijay* looked at him bewildered. Wondering what was going on.

Divya's father put out his hand for a handshake, which *Vijay* obliged.

"Happy birthday Viay Amarnath and I am Vijayandranath, and little princess and I shall take leave for we need to clarify certain things and settle a messy situation outside." He said to *Vijay* and *Divya*.

"What about present for my daddy, grandpa?" Pranavi asked him innocently.

"Divya..." was all he said aloud and turned his attention towards Pranavi, *"It will take some time, so meanwhile let's leave amma and daddy to talk. What do you say little princess? Did he get you chocolate delight milkshake?"* Pranavi shook her head negatively.

"He didn't is it; he is going to die for not getting the order right. Now where is my ironman sword." he said walking out of the room, shutting the door quietly.

Pranavi's happy giggle could be heard, as she corrected him, ironman doesn't have a sword.

CHAPTER III

Always

Rubina looked at her father with dejection in her eyes. She was shocked to see him.

Prior to the knock on the door, *Rubina* was subjected to bruises for answering back to her husband. She had returned from a client's house cursing her fate after delivering the stitched dresses and blouses in time.

Tailoring was her only source of livelihood. She looked at the posh apartment with sadness as she waited for her client to pay her.

She didn't know the value of living in comfort before her marriage. She always felt she deserved the best. She remembered her tantrums and whims that she threw around her parents' house. taking things for granted. Now she understood the importance of what they were providing.

The maid of the house stood guard near the door, making sure Rubina wouldn't enter the house when the madam went in to get her purse. The state she was in, she knew that's how people would see her.

She didn't blame the maid; with the crime rate going up people needed to be cautious.

If only she had completed her studics in time. The education she had was subjected only as a medium of communication. She was grateful to the maid, for every day after finishing her household chores and fetching water from the municipal lorry. She would walk over to the nearby apartments and ask for tailoring work. During one such time the maid spotted her and gave her small jobs like fitting or stiches removal. Slowly she saw better days with little more orders following. She was in debt to the maid *Saritha*. That was her name. *Rubina* addressed her as *Saritha didi*.

The amount received gave her a relief, that this month's rent could be paid in time and she could save up for a few groceries also pay the monthly installment for the sewing machine.

The festival was nearing and she wished for a decent meal which seemed a faraway dream in their circumstances. But festival gave her hope for in the given circumstances Tailors were in demand and *Rubina* was banking on making ends meet by taking up orders.

Fate seemed to have another card up its sleeve.

Her husband was already standing by the locked door of their rented house, more of a single room, which had partitions veiled by her chunnis thrown carefully over thin ropes. That divided it into a kitchen at a corner, and sleeping place in the further end. She had placed their suitcases which at a particular time had seen good days. It was used as a makeshift dressing table. A small hand mirror was dangling precariously on the wall.

"Where did you go?" he asked her eyeing her hands which clutched a purse.

"Here only, Shabnam's house." she lied, and fumbled with the house keys.

"Oh..." he replied.

He tried to take the keys from her hand and *Rubina* in fright let go of her purse. A few notes were seen. She panicked and picked it up. But *Abdul* was a cunning fellow his eyes caught sight of the money.

"Shabnam gave you money, is it?"

"No- that's for the material. I took up a new order." She said and the lock gave way just then, she blew out air in anxiety. She walked in scared and looked around for a safe place to hide her purse.

"Give me the cash now Rubina, I know you took a loan in the bank, under the small sc ale industry loan and planning to rent a shop for your tailoring." He said with a rough tone of voice.

"Where is that money?" he asked her threateningly.

"Please not this time, I need to pay the rent which we are behind from several months, also get materials too. I cannot give you the money this time. I need to set up the tailoring shop. I worked very hard for it."

"Are you crazy, if I invest now in the coming future, we can buy better houses and give them for rent." Her husband *Abdul* said trying to convince her.

She caught the money tight at her bosom and refused.

"No, I cannot give you money, you've already sold my ornaments and wasted a lot of amount on business proposals, at least I working so you got a roof on your head and food to eat once in a day."

"Are you trying to accuse me of stealing, where is that bank book, give me the cheque now." he slapped her hard.

Trying to let go from his clutch she blurted out, *"There is no cheque only money."*

"Ah, so you stashed away from my eyes is it, give it to me right now or else will kill you."

He caught her hair and dragged her on the floor. The ruffian was so brutal he used his feet to kick her for talking back.

"it's your bad luck that has fallen on me. if only I had not married you. stupid female." He spat on her.

"Seeing your dressing style and all I thought you were from a rich family. To attract you I had to take a lot of hand loans. You think those gifts came for free is it and movie tickets cost a bomb. Fancy restaurant dinners. Bike rides, do you even know how much petrol costs are? You fell for them and now you act as if I wasted all that money. Even you were my investment. A wasted investment like you said earlier." Saying he kicked her with his leg again.

"Now hand over the money you took loan from the bank." He said threateningly to her.

She didn't let go of her purse, which he tried to snatch. In that process he fractured her finger that was clutching the purse dearly.

She doubled up in pain. *"I will not give you the money, you'll drink it all up and waste it on prostitutes."*

"Shut up and hand it over." He screamed on her face and hit her.

She cursed herself for believing him and running away on the day of her *Nikah*.

The shower of beatings coming towards her, reminded her of her parents and their warnings. She had turned deaf to their words and was now facing the consequences. She threw him aside with all her might and ran towards the door to save herself from the beatings.

There was a knock, *Rubina* blindly opened the door to whoever it was and stood still facing her father.

"Who is it, did you savior come to take you away?" Abdul asked her mockingly. He held a rod in his hand and gestured at her to comeback and hand over the cash.

"Give me the cash and leave with your savior my bad investment."

She faced her father in silence and he looked at the state se was in with fiery eyes.

It hurt him that *Abdul* with whom she had run away three years back for a bright future, was hurling abusive words at her. all these years he was angry she had run away on her *Nikah* and her family faced the wrath of society and their gossips. Rubina had no idea that her mother had been hospitalized in that process. *Rubina's* father was angry initially but later softened for she was his only child. He decided to search for and it took hm three years to find out where she lived. And now seeing her in this state his blood boiled.

She tried to cover her hands with her chunni, but her father had seen enough.

Her husband *Abdul* had rewarded her all these years with a bruised body. Her decision was wrong, but so was *Rubina's* father. He should not have waited till now.

Rubina felt ashamed to face the man who brought her up like a princess.

"So, this is the life you choose to be with, refusing the future I wanted to give you?"

His angered voice resonated around the house. she couldn't answer him.

"You've no business to interfere in my family life, she's no longer your daughter." Abdul shouted at *Rubina's* father. and pointed towards the front door indicating that he needed to leave.

Rubina, whose eyes welled up not for her pain but to see a face she had always admired from the time she could recognize and understand the world.

Mazar Khan, her father didn't say anything and turned on his heel to walk away.

He stopped as he neared the front door and with his back still facing them, he spoke up again,

"I raised a tigress in my family, as far as my knowledge goes, she would not let even a fly hurt me neither anyone speak back rudely."

Mazar Khan lifted his head high and his voice seemed even louder, *"I have been waiting near my door for that tigress to return home. And today waiting outside your door."*

He then stepped out of her house, he heard a loud slap and *Mazar Khan's* hand was interlocked with *Rubina's.* His heart soared in pride as his daughter followed him back home.

Mazar Khan knew what had happened cannot be undone. He was going to make sure that this memory of hers is but a fading lesson like a little girl learning the bicycle. He would make sure the falls will be deleted, and the triumph of riding the bicycle successfully would be remembered. He will not let her cry because of the incidents that have stained her, but let her wash them off as a lesson and move on.

Children including elders tend to commit mistakes, that doesn't mean chapter ended, game over. Remember it's not over until it's over.

CHAPTER IV

Unexpected Advice

"Marriage drifts friends apart and we fall into duties, hardly having time to keep in touch. And when we get a chance to meet up, we make sure it's the teenagers that are present and not the real aged people." Jhansi casually stated sipping her coffee.

She suddenly felt as if she delivered a motivating dialogue.

Jhansi waited for an appreciation from *Aparna*, who was preoccupied hardly listening to her.

"This girl I tell you." Jhansi shook her head unbelievingly, at Aparna.

Aparna had entered the café exhausted, and placed her purchased items on the table helping herself to a nearby chair. She filled it with shopping bags, before settling down and that's when she started off with her questions to *Jhansi*.

"Heard your having a dinner date today. Meher told me. He was like cracking up saying the kindergarten Jhansi that's what he called you throughout the phone conversation every time he mentioned your name." Aparna giggled whenever the kindergarten word came up. *"Kindergarten my my what names he chooses."*

She helped herself with a French fry, *"Hmm just what I wanted, you didn't add the peri peri girl."* She said with a scorn face and put the contents into the packet provided, tore the small peri peri sachets added the masala to French fries before shaking them well. *Aparna* then transferred it to the plate.

"That's how you've got to eat baby, what's the use maintaining a cookery show when you hardly know the basics dear." Aparna mocked Jhansi.

Jhansi let out a sigh and decided to keep quiet instead of replying. *Aparna* was one helluva of girl to handle and she was in no mood to argue with her, though it would be a friendly banter.

Aparna felt the café was unusually silent though it did have the usual walk ins and people in conversation at the tables.

"Why is the café silent and why are all the people whispering?" she leaned towards *Jhansi* asking in a secretive manner.

Jhansi who was sitting opposite to her *blew* outair, *"Why do I have to put up with this crazy girl god."* She said to herself.

Jhansi stopped herself from saying anything cynical aloud and let her thoughts be, she leaned forward reaching out, to remove *Aparna's* Bluetooth.

"That's why." She said and signaled for her to help herself with the right side, *Jhansi* placed the left ear piece on the table.

"Oh, yeah, my bad I was on call with Meher like I was telling you earlier and then I remembered to I said I will catch up with you here in the café. You know what? How will you know it was between Meher and me. So, Meher was telling me about your dinner date. I think I did ask you earlier about it and you didn't answer me." Aparna satirically said to Jhansi.

"Gosh girl what did I do to be your family member, don't you even give a chance to the other person to reply and when they do your in another universe totally."

"God's gift you could say bhakta." Aparna winked at her and made a pose of an Indian deity.

"Shut up okay, it's the other way round."

"Are you done with your coffee?" Aparna asked her, checking her messages in the phone.

"I was warming up to it. Why are you not going to get one for yourself? Shall I take up an order for you? I just ordered French fries and was waiting. So, why did you ask for me to come here?" Jhansi asked her sister – in -law.

"Nope I am not in a mood for coffee, but these fries are all for me right."

"Help yourself."

"I have parlor appointment and also a date. Unlike your Meher it's a handsome guy and I really needed to doll up for him so you see, I cannot go around with these packages. I knew you'll be coming over to

pick up Anjali so I asked you over to the café." Aparna blinked her eyes several times and threw her a society pose.

"Save your elite stuff to the handsome you're going to meet. I am done with the coffee, how did you come?" Jhansi asked her, she used a tissue to wipe her hand and got up to leave.

"Cab."

"Okay then I will first drop you off at the beauty parlor. It's your regular Styles and care parlor, right?" Jhansi enquired.

"Yep, that's the one." Aparna gave her a thumbs up.

"Fine then, That's on the way to Anjali's school. I've got good ten minutes more until her home bell goes." Jhansi helped Aparna with the packages.

"It's okay I can manage." Aparna said to her.

"Fine then." Jhansi said, letting go of the packages.

"Girl that's mean, you're supposed to offer help, even though I say it's okay."

"Oh, really." Jhansi said mockingly.

"Where are your manners gosh, that oh really sounds so cheap coming from you." Aparna complained.

"Cut the chase darling, I did offer to drop you, what should I do when you try to behave sassy."

"Okay now let's go."

Back in the car, *Aparna* out of the blue questioned her, *"I watched your recent episode, noticed your subscribers are reaching up."*

Jhansi nodded her head but did not reply, her concentration was on the driving.

"I envy you're doing something; I wish I could also come up with an idea that gives me an identity. Anyways I am happy like this." Aparna said, while she opened up a video of *Jhansi's* in the YouTube.

"I was happy too at one point of time. After you get married that's when you realize you want to get back in touch with yourself. You'll miss that person who had ideas stashed away at every nook and corner in her personal space. You'll hardly find time for personal space. Not that you have trouble in paradise. You just become a wife, daughter in law and mother. Your name and the person you were fade out."

"Hmm, exactly." Aparna said hardly listening to *Jhansi's* words.

Jhansi smiled at her innocence; *Aparna* her husband Meher's younger sibling was six years younger to her. proposals were streaming recently, for she had asked her parents time till she was done with her MBA.

Aparna was a darling, she always seemed preoccupied but that was just her outer version. That girl had a sharp mind and when time calls for it, she would give you the most amazing advice.

She remembered the incident three years back when *Jhansi* and *Aparna* were shopping at the central, for a certain cousin's engagement. *Jhansi* met up with her schoolmate *Sujatha*.

After the hugs and oh my god.

I cannot believe it's you.

Just look at you my my!

The usual conversation between friends who get to see each other after a long time.

After exchange of pleasantries, they drove over to a restaurant and sat down comfortably to catch up over lunch.

The order was placed.

Jhansi and *Sujatha* started catching on the lost days.

Aparna was busy with her mobile after the introductions were made.

"I could've gone home nah, you girls need your time to catch up." Aparna said, trying to give them space.

"Come on now you're not a bother in-between us." Sujatha said, making her feel comfortable with her. *"And you called me a girl that's priceless."*

"And by the way, don't you want juicy bits of info on your sister-in-law. Madam was a cat in school and had them boys drool over her." *Sujatha* said winking at her.

"All ears, I don't mind if Jhansi leaves. let's talk. What say Jhansi baby. Deal okay nah." She joked with *Jhansi*.

Jhansi playfully hit her on her head, *"As if you are innocent, everyone has their masti time when they are growing up."* *Jhansi* said and sighed.

Sujatha too sighed.

"Those days were really something." Both chorused and looked at each other shouting *"Jinx."* They said aloud and started laughing.

"Remember how we used to funnily call each other in school."

"Yeah, hey my girl come here."

"My girl what is your name?"

And remember *Kamakshi* ma'am our math teacher when she got angry, *"Hey my girl stand up on the bench out of my class."*

"Seriously and Avani ma'am please class answer me silently."

"How about this one, do you remember all the teachers praising us as you are the worst batch they've ever taught."

"Mrs Savitha famous line talk girl I cannot hear my voice, she was so puny and how she used to go around with that big scale scaring us."

"I loved Cassandra miss da, she was a darling and Mrs.Mason what a fright she used to give us during assembly and when we got caught with nail polish."

"Don't forget Mrs. Alice, our singing teacher, where you in the school choir?" Sujatha asked *Jhansi*, to which she nodded her head and suddenly both the ladies broke into a school song.

"If there is something to say, say it now.

If there is something to do, do it now. now before it is too late,

And they forgot the lines after that, Sujatha and Jhansi realized their surroundings. They felt embarrassed seeing the waiter who was gaping at them wide eyed with the food platter in his hand.

Aparna who was typing in her mobile looked up at them wondering, *"Whoa what's happening?"*

Suddenly a lady from the opposite table joined in and completed the school song and another person joined from a little bit further table.

"Now is the time for every good thing.

Do not wait until tomorrow,

For tomorrow maybe a little too late."

The occupied tables audience were watching them and suddenly they started clapping.

"Good old days...keep the memory alive ladies." Someone from the restaurant appreciated them.

"Yeah, that was one of our assembly song too, which school did you'll go too?" someone else called out.

"Thank you for that cheerful reminder." A middle-aged man reciprocated, I completely forgot how life used to be hanging out with friends.

It took a while for everyone to settle back into their places. The mood in the restaurant felt vibrant and cheerful.

Sujatha and *Jhansi* started giggling like school girls and whispering about what happened just now.

"That was something right." Sujatha said pushing her hair back that kept falling on her face for she was doubling up unable to stop her laughter.

"I should add you in our school group, many were asking about you, share your number." Sujatha said *to Jhansi* and added her in the WhatsApp school group.

"Seriously I needed that yaar been itching to sing the songs we learnt back then in school." She said and her eyes welled up in happiness.

Both fell silent. *Aparna* looked at them wondering why they both seemed sad.

"Hey girls what's wrong you both were all excited and singing and now what's the gloom atmosphere for? Looks like a dark cloud is hovering over you'll." She tried to snap them off their silence.

Jhansi was still silent but *Sujatha* answered, *"Life was awesome then. You know what Aparna we had such crazy ideas to start our own business. We wanted to be someone, yes, I am sure Jhansi is happy and well settled in her married life like me. We get to go on vacations, movies and other stuff too. but that girl spark is no longer there. That I am so and so, well it's not there. We are under the shadow of our surnames or husband's names. When time called us to do something we were busy with our kids and other things. Now when we want to do something, age has caught up and middle age is screaming I don't think so."*

Aparna clapped her hands and shot out her sarcasm, *"Wow that was one sob story you came out with. For a second I felt I was watching a black and white film."*

"Shut up Aparna." Jhansi tried to cut her off.

"No-no you girls shut up for once, look around you. which world are you living in. damn man when a colonel can come up with a fried chicken idea at the age of sixty what's with you two sobbing up stories. I mean look at you. Use the resources you have to an advantage and break the walls you both have placed around you. what's with you churning out dramas saying our life is over and stuff like that. I mean look at you. looking at the way you dress and designer clothes, bag etc you can do something with that talent of yours. And Jhansi how our relatives appreciate your cooking. Crazy man she can make the most delicious food with minimal ingredients available. These restaurant foods are no match to her culinary skills. Open your eyes girls and kick out that self-pity your people are brooding over."

Aparna wanted to add more and then looked at their surprised faces, *"Oops I did take it a bit far, ladies in case you felt I burned your ego, well I am pretty much fine with it. But think it over. Okay. Change is not indecision. First get that right."*

Aparna picked up her backpack, *"Okay then I've got to go. My wolf pack is around the corner. Will be back home by seven Jhansi, cover for me girl. It was a pleasure meeting you Sujatha."* She shook her hand and added, *"Next time when I get an invite to meet up with you, hoping at your business place."* She smiled and literally ran.

Jhansi remembered she was thinking of ways to apologize to *Sujatha. Aparna* could be a tab bit straight forward and she hardly worried if the person facing her was receiving it well. She always said her bit and never bothered the consequences. Relatives were vary of her when they came home and kept their conversations minimal with her.

"Suja..."

"That sister-in-law of yours is a piece."

"Yeah, I know and I am sorry for her talk down to you."

"Are you kidding she opened my eyes, what the hell are you doing with such a bomb at your place. Do you have a pen, I have a paper somewhere ah...here I think this bill invoice will do for moment. Now push the food aside. Wait a minute are you hungry? No nah then fine this is more important."

That's how they came up with their career ideas.

'Can a thank you ever fill the bag of gratitude she had for Aparna.' Jhansi thought to herself and smiled hearing her voice playing back as she explained how to prepare *Kashmiri pulav. Aparna* had clicked on her video.

"More than the pulav I liked the bread pizza you posted three days back. My friends wanted me to thank you on their behalf for the easy snack item with ingredients that were home friendly."

"Noted, so did anyone pass on suggestions like last time you mentioned, they wanted to try out easy cake recipes right?" Jhansi asked and pressed the right indicator button, whilst she took a turn.

Her mobile vibrated with a notification.

"There I posted their requests in your WhatsApp, check it out when you're free. And madam you owe me, I think at least ten more of my friends subscribed to your channel and hit the bell notification today."

"Thanks, my darling sister – in -law, tell what can I do for all the help you give me."

"Pay my credit card bill that's enough." Aparna turned towards her excitedly and asked her.

"Aww that's hardly a favor and if I pay your bill I am sure you'll not like it. So let me cook something special for you tomorrow." Jhansi teased Aparna as she stopped the car.

"Stingy girl, now why did you stop the car now?" Aparna asked her.

"Because, your destination has arrived." Jhansi replied winking at her.

"Okay then I will leave my packages in the car, anyways after picking up Anjali you'll be heading home right. Ask Lakshmi to leave them in my room." Aparna got off and waved a bye to Jhansi. She walked towards the three storied building. She suddenly jumped up in

joy and threw a blowing kiss towards *Jhansi* who waved back at her and started the car ignition. She placed the phone aside after transferring an amount to *Aparna*.

Jhansi eased the car out and drove to *Anjali's* play school. Her car stereo playing the song *Aurora*, and *Jhansi* told herself, well my *Aurora* is you, *Aparna*!

Sometimes destinations feel they've ended. It takes the person who has travelled to understand that there is no final destination, but only roads to travel and stop around for a while. Always remember that a begin you have to dare the first step!

CHAPTER V

Umbrella

DearAmma,

Every time I close my eyes, I remember you Amma. And then when my eyes are open, I see you in everything that I encounter. It's like you are still with me.

Is only a physical presence called a presence? and not an invisible one? I don't think so.

Many criticize me saying it's my mind conjuring up the talks I have with you, subconsciously. I would like to prove them wrong.

Then again what do I gain by proving them wrong? but an acknowledgement.

Will it change anything?

Will it make me happier?

Well, I am happy with you in me, that's fair enough and that's all I want.

So, cutting out the sentimental stuff to the real reason for me to pen this letter today, to you Amma is because I see myself as a failure. Like the trend goes I would be defined under #failure (that's read hashtag failure Amma). I even wrote a poem describing the state of mind I am drifting in. would you like to hear it? You always do no matter what work you were in and I am sure you wouldn't say no to me this time too. So, this is how it goes...

It's been a while I took a break, from my regular time-controlled list of do's.

I realized I am but human, and could feel the pain given.

Mind you for I did mention, given not shared!

Alas, that's the irony I let myself be.

I then again realized, taking a break from crowd is momentary to play with thoughts,

Thoughts I had taken from them that defined me?

Was it necessary? Right now, I think a big NO,

Pity me, it was on my priority list when they spoke and I felt it then.

I pushed myself into the dearth of hopelessness.

I distanced myself and became the gargoyle of nothing I am painted in.

Time lapsed; the days swept by.

I am but drifting by, on the plank of life I perch myself and brave the sea,

Who still surrounds me with its turbulent advice.

I enjoy my solitude, then again, I need my crowd to breath, feel and sense life again!

Am I waiting for a savior?

Will one come by?

Let me be frank, until one decides they want to saved, the mist that is a blanket to the eyes will not be pulled back to be seen.

Again and again, I habituate to turn myself to an on and off approach.

I reason answering my opinionated mind, 'Well isn't life all about changes that make one adapt to survive?

Again, I shall and again I will, no matter what,

Until the time comes. That stances me not to give in to the temptation of defeat.

I am but my own umbrella, and under the harshness of weather I shall but spend time in solitude to recoup and revert into a main stream life called world.

Why did I write those words Amma? Because I felt the criticism creep into my bones. They felt brittle and I shattered myself chaining my independence to failure. I wanted to do something. But something is not what one does right Amma? No, we don't choose something because we have to. Knowingly we walk the path we are inclined. Yet, as the toe hits a pebble the tremors it sends across our body, we let it sink in, and we take a momentary break.

Why?

Because we show the world 'See I am hurt.'

I am hurt Amma. I remember telling you during our final encounter and your reply was, 'SO!'

I still can feel that word hit me hard on my face till date.

When I citied reasons why I was in depression and I let the world engulf me. you listened to me patiently and then uttered a single syllable 'SO!'

What did you mean when you questioned me 'SO?' I was telling you why I could not do it? because I am busy doing my chores. And then again you did lend your ears to my lamentations and replied with a 'SO!' This word caught me irritated.

"I have problems," *I literally screamed and you calmly said,* **"So does everyone."** *and continued with whatever you were doing.*

What were you trying to imply? my chaotic mind was finding excuses to reply to the SO! You kept throwing back at me.

It was like, like we were playing table tennis and no matter how rogue a shot I sent assuming you to be a fragile partner you equally returned it to me with ease, with the utterance of 'SO!'

This conversation I remember distinctly went on for a couple of minutes and I gave in vexed. Those words of dejection I threw at you amma.

"Fine you win I lose. I cannot be what you wanted me to be. Just let me survive in the world till my breath lasts. I appreciate I can be hands on for my family and do the necessary bit of everyday chores."

I was patronizing my work without sparring u thought that I spelt in that way, for I was churning up excuses and finding ways to explain how much I do and don't have time to be what you wanted me to be Amma.

I can still clearly visualize your grin when you decided to stop teasing me and instead lecture me.

'Be mindful of your thoughts, all is creation.' *You said to me.*

The memory of my quizzical expression I shared trying to make out where the conversation was leading to still lingers fresh in me.

Amma, I had enough of people telling me I am not qualified to be what I was doing. I cannot take anymore criticism. I am breaking up and I feel that's enough. Why should I forge ahead into a world that hardly acknowledges me and is bent to show my faults at my face. I feel broken Amma. I cannot build strong walls or a house at the bricks thrown at me, neither make lemon juice. That's what motivation speaks and I give a damn to them words. I've decided to quit and lead a life unseen. Why do I need to flatter myself to prove I am this or that?

I always threw these questions at you and still flaunt around them when I get into the dark mood. You've had your answer ready then and now. When I say now, it's because I rewind the conversation, I had with you to pull back from the abyss I jump into immediately when I find myself attacked. That safety string, I hang on to, when I allow myself to be pulled down are the words you shared with me. you can call it my session, therapy with you forever, for **'Collaborative mindset helps me achieve a better perspective.'**

'Collaborative mindset for a better perspective' *I liked the way you coined it. I sat there with a hot cup of coffee you had brewed just the way I preferred. And then it was a single sided conversation from you.*

"Let me remind you a few lines you might have heard it before, it's not my original quote but borrowed from the famous poet Khalil Gibran song lyrics 'On children'.

Your children are not your children
They are the sons and daughter of life's longing for itself
They come through you but not from you
And though they are with you yet they belong not to you.

Why did I recite these lines to you, let me explain. Everyone is assigned to do their duty or work according to their perspective. But assumptions thrown that you have to inch only till a certain limit is what I call foolishness. When born you are on your back, but only for a few days you learnt to turn on sides, then roll. It didn't stop there because it tires you to repeat the same process day in and out, you needed to explore to tire the thoughts what if? you needed to push yourself to crawl, stand and walk.

Same applies to the **'WHAT IF'** *you want to prioritize to do something you feel you can. The society didn't implore you with ideas* *you need to do. They were your own. You felt them. You wanted to identify with them. When someone criticizes you, take it. Just because it hurts you or depresses you people are not going to stop. And then if you stop what you wanted to do it's not going to stop those mouths from commenting.*

it criticized when you didn't do well, afterwards it will comment that never tried and left in mid-way. It's a two-sided coin. I didn't say double edged sword mind you. A coin has its own version.

Now coming to the topic criticism if you are taking it to heart, well its good.

Write down their suggestions and what are the fingers pointing at.

Why do you want to give in to their fancies and whims?

Are you waiting for someone to protect you with an umbrella?

You shade yourself from harsh weather and other things carrying your own umbrella and opening it up when necessary to protect yourself.

Be your own umbrella, stop expecting help and de-motivating yourself because someone said something. If you give up that's your fault do not blame it on others. Stop self-loathing, and this drama of self-pity and craving for sympathy.

I remember the way you looked at me when you asked me this question Amma.

Did I ask you to become something? I don't think so!

I gave you an education and let you choose your path. I asked if you wanted to get married and then proceeded. When you pursued what you wanted to do, I felt happy. Now giving up on something I will but nod my head. I can only suggest like others so tell me once again why should I not ask you when you tell me, "Amma I am hurt so I am giving up on my dream."

It was your dream. Or was it mine? I reminded you time and again when you lamented, I want to become something; this was your dream. So, let me correct you it was not my dream you are giving up on but yours, am I right or AM I RIGHT?

Oh, please don't even add a term to your giving up. Calling it Procrastination and its anxiety related. You've hiked up on the stress levels so your behavior is bizarre and need rest. That's pure giving up. Procrastination is NOT laziness, its but an emotion you are toying around with. Citing "I am feeling anxious, my anxiety is stopping me from doing anything."

Oh, for God's sake grow up. Break yourself from that repetitive cycle leaving things half way. Every time you run does not garner a win-win. Losing also boosts up with what you went comfortable with. Don't tell me you have forgotten the Hare and tortoise story which I told you and probably heard during your school or now on social media pages. Look at me and answer me, WHAT DID YOU WANT TO BECOME, AND DID BEFORE THE CRITISIM CAUGHT YOU OFF BALANCE.

I faced her with hesitation and spoke back with a clear mind.

Tara closed the book she was narrating from and looked at the anxious faces watching her with bated breath. The school auditorium was silent, and the only sound heard was the gentle whirring of the fan. A student from the seventh grade broke the silence questioning Tara.

"What did you answer your Amma when she motivated you back to be what you wanted to be ma'am?"

Tara looked the student with an expressive smile. "Do you really want to know how not to let depression get into you and criticism break you?"

The whole Auditorium including the faculty and other staff members chorused with a big yes. The principal too was inquisitive to hear what answer Tara had given to her amma.

She had taken them on a sojourn along with her into her story.

Tara a renowned Author and storyteller, was invited as a chief guest to 'Anna Maria Convent' for their silver jubilee anniversary stood silent at the podium. She had been invited to motivate them to their future and what better way then delivering a speech to the youngsters about dejection, depression, criticism and failure. She smiled watching their enthusiastic faces and resumed her narration.

"This is what I told her, when she asked me what was my dream?"

The auditorium resonated with her voice in every corner and her words found home in the hearts of the listeners. She smiled to herself for she felt her invisible umbrella's being shared and each was understanding that they need to open theirs if they want to fight the world that compliments them with negativity.

"My dream was to become a writer. (I did manage to stream into becoming). I wanted to give a place to the lesser-known people I keep encountering in daily basis who feel a worthlessness and survive because they need to. My goal was to imagine them that they're the leading character in their own adventure. I wanted to become a writer that writes for them, about them and still maintain an aura that it's a story of fiction with realism hidden in-between lines."

Tara stopped and watched, not that their expressions mattered she was reliving her moments with her mother. Her Amma who had passed on twelve years back and still Tara feels her presence when she finds herself in a spot. Right now, she could see her vividly sitting in her vacant chair and listening to her.

"When your young people often ask you what is your dream? But as you get older less people ask you about your dream. The world makes it hard for the adult in you to pave a path towards the dream. Reality creates a distance between you and your dreams and it gradually becomes insignificant. Suddenly you find you've forgotten about it altogether.

A reminder is all you need.

Before, I completely forgot about my dream, I was lucky my Amma reminded me about it. She didn't push me or chide me neither did she mock me. she reminded me.

It was me who opened up my umbrella so that I could start dreaming again. because, I realized something, maybe I was the one who held myself back and considered myself as a nobody.

Grounded by reality, I tended to give up easily. I wonder if I was one who turned off my own spotlight.

People say that life is not a fairy tale. But, sometimes like a child or a fool maybe we should dream of a world that exists only in fairy tales.

Remember if one doesn't turn off their spotlight,

If one never gives up on their dreams,

Then one can pursue and create their own fairy tale by achieving one's dream.

The satisfaction of you've tried is worth more. I will not say money because to survive one needs money, its ground reality, I would be thrown to a mental hospital if I go around saying money is not important for survival.

Never forget to try what you wanted to be, if you fail and people voice out negativity. Care a dime and try it again. it's never over until it's over!

The Auditorium seemed silent, to Tara they seemed spell bound.

"Before I leave can I tell you a small secret of mine?"

The crowd didn't object and she obliged them.

"Let people judge you, allow them to misunderstand you. even gossip about you. because, listen to me very carefully WHAT THEY THINK ABOUT YOU ISN'T YOUR PROBLEM. Their opinions are not going to feed you, pay bills or achieve your goals for you. NO MATTER WHAT THEY DO OR SAY. NEVER EVER DOUBT YOUR WORTH.

The standing ovation she received still resounded in her ears after leaving the premises.

Tara opened her designer purse and pulled out a well-worn notebook paper she had written a letter to her Amma twelve years back when she had passed on.

A memory that spelt love and strength.

*She read the last line, **"Miracles do come in your way, you need to welcome them with confidence."** The words her Amma had told her time and again. she folded it back neatly and replaced it in her purse. Tara looked out of the car window the sun was setting greeting nature and exchanging about events of the day that was spent. it went ahead to rest. Not forever but to re-energize and shine again with enthusiasm the next day.*

Sometimes you need to take a break, but not give up.

Thank you for reading a memory I love in a short story form titled UMBRELLA. This is Tara, Taramaniratnam signing off until next time.

CHAPTER VI

Privacy?

Vikrant smiled when he heard his wife *Ira* complain that she had to make biryani on Sunday.

"Why cannot we order it Vicky? Come on I deserve a break too. Yaar, lets chill by going out for lunch. Then catch a movie, good idea nah what do you say?" Ira gave him a cute innocent look, twisting the napkin in her hands as she spoke to him. Ira looked irresistible in her *purple baby doll lingerie*, and Vikrant was unable to concentrate on the printed words.

Vikrant threw his newspaper aside signaled to her to come to him and when she did, he hugged her. She snuggled to him, and he pushed her loose hair back. Her hair held the fragrance of roses, she must have used a hair spray he thought. He was about to kiss her tempting bare neck when his mobile rang cutting their romance short. He ignored it and pulled her closer, the mobile stopped its interruption and he brushed his lips on her neck, his touch gave her a giggling spell. She squeezed his waistline with both her hands in intimacy. The phone decided to break their romance no matter what probably it was jealous watching them together and rang again.

Ira, *Vikrant's* wife pushed him aside and picked up his mobile offended to share a piece of her mind.

"Damn this mobile, does it not know Sunday calls for privacy?"

Vikrant realized it was his mobile she was handling and suddenly let out a, *"Hey that's my mobile."*

"Yes, I know it's your mobile Vicky. Its Dhanu calling so I answered. Why am I not supposed to touch your mobile?"

He didn't answer the question *Ira* threw at him with a smug. His memory suddenly hit him hard. The word PRIVACY made him feel guilt. He remembered the incident that had happened during his college days.

• • •

Vikrant's grandfather chuckled when he saw his grandson's status in Facebook.

He read Vikrant's statement out loud to Vikrant's mother and father.

"Annoyed with my mother for answering a call on my mobile, no privacy at home."

Vikrant stared hard at his grandfather, who was sitting across the dining table.

His daughter -in- law served him another roti in silence.

Vikrant's father pulled a chair and sat down with an amused look, hearing his father read out the words. "*Interesting.*" Was all he said.

He knew his father was not the kind to let things slide easily. So, the evening dinner will definitely see a drama.

He looked at his wife who was serving dinner in silence, "*I got the paneer packet along with milk. Let me know now only what you want as there is still time for the shop to close. Tomorrow I will be leaving early to office.*"

"*No that's fine, nothing I want as of now.*" Vikrant's mother replied and walked back to the kitchen.

"*Peace of mind I think she needs.*" Vikrant's grandfather *Yadav* said wittily.

"*Dad come on now.*" Vikrant's father *Santhosh* tried to cut his father's wise cracks.

"*I only replied for her, you asked what else she needs and i spoke as her spokesperson. You know Viji never asks you anything for herself except things for the house. what's wrong if I reply.*" Vikrant's father *Yadav* watched his son getting irritated.

"*Oh, really gramps, so you think what I posted was wrong. I was watching television and she picked up my friends call. Can you beat that. How can mom do that? Seriously. My mobile is off limits gramps. Just imagine. I know when to receive and answer my calls.*"

The accusation, made his mother's heart cringe and she wondered, "Am *I guilty? Don't I have a right to talk to his friends? I am family too. it was dhanu his friend who is like a son to me. don't I have a right to answer a call from a known person? are my son's friends off limit to me.*

Yadav, *Vikrant's* grandfather helped himself with a generous ladle of curry and watched his daughter -in -law *Viji's* expression, she was contemplating on the incident that had happened between her and her adolescent son.

Yadav replied, *"Yes, son the party is guilty, for buying the phone of your choice, foregoing a few of her wishes to keep you happy and in par with the society status, she doesn't object to sleepovers or late nights. Sometimes the movies attended bunking classes I wonder from whom you receive the amount? Those trendy clothes and other whims of your's though late get to be fulfilled. You are absolutely right and I agree you have the liberty to post about your private matter, of her picking up your call of your friend whom she treats like her own son when you were beyond reach and..."*

He let the **AND** word hang icily and continued after a few seconds of painful silence,

"And you post a private incident on your social media that you've no privacy. What's this Garima, oh! You made Biryani for your privacy son it's his favorite dish right...nice. If I am not mistaken you answered the call of Dhanu to invite him over for biryani."

Vikrant's memory bubble was popped with *Ira* tellinghim, *"It was Dhanu who called you. he told me he is getting your mom over here to our apartment for she made biryani for you and not to prepare lunch. Let's cancel the outing then Vicks."*

Vikrant didn't answer her.

It was a memory with a slight sting.

some memories maybe laced with a hiccup. That doesn't make it bad. But paves a path to make another happy one. All one has to do is to remember the lesson it taught and forget the hurt of the incident.

CHAPTER VII

This is love

Mukitha excitedly opened her present, her happy face turned grim and she roughly placed the package with a thud on the dining table. *Vijji*, that's Vijayalakshmi, she felt it was too big for her sweet short height and preferred to be called *Vijji*.

She was busy with her evening snack preparation. Her concentration was on her tab which she had masterly placed on the empty bowl as a makeshift stand on the dining table. Her tab slipped and slid down from its position, with *Mukitha's* disappointment shown on the received package.

Vijji was trying to make **'Garlic Bread'**. Mukitha looked up at her mother.

"Nothing... you make garlic bread, pizza and what not with loads of cheese, mayonnaise and everything for your Rajabeta Namit." She said with a scorn.

"What's wrong with your expression Mukhi I think you lost it when coming back from college." Her mother teased her.

Vijji looked at her preparation and mentally made note of everything, garlic finely chopped, coriander cut for garnish, butter melted, oregano and chili flakes added along with salt. Her eyes now roamed to catch where she placed her bread packet. She found it sitting on the other end of the dinning table.

"Mukhi pass the bread nah, I need to dice them." She asked her daughter for help.

Which was not reciprocated when the request was placed with a loving tone. *Vijji* repeated her sentence, a bit louder that the maid in the kitchen doing the vessels heard it too. *Mukhi* who by now had walked over to the sitting room, slopped herself on the sofa and surfed the channels with no intention of watching television.

"Alright, that's it..." *Vijji* made a louder statement.

Mukhi knew she had taken a bit far, involuntarily her legs took her towards where the bread was and her hands picked up the bread. She gave it to her mother.

"Okay what's the deal of all this drama, drama queen." Vijji asked her daughter as she opened the bread packet and placed the bread on the chopping tray to cut out the edges.

Mukhi took time to answer her mother back.

"Okay leave it, suit yourself." Vijji said for she didn't want to throw more attention to her daughter's trivial attention seeking.

"This..." Mukitha said showing her mother what she received from her brother as a Rakhi gift.

She had received an expensive makeup kit, hairbands, nail paint and other accessories with loads of chocolate bars.

"Nice... should appreciate Namit for his effort." The mother in *Vijji* was happy that her son for once had not consulted her but purchased the *Rakhi* gift on his own for his sister. She remembered the previous *Rakhi* encounters which was always a last-minute gift furnished from *Vijji's* side, for she knew *Namit* would forget to get one for his sister. This year was really special. he remembered.

"What nice...I was expecting the latest phone and I get this..." Mukhi dug her hand to fish out the presents. Her miffed expression, changed. *Vijji* who had cut up all her bread pieces into the required shape knit her brows watching her daughters sudden change of exprtession that went from anger, to surprise and then a broad grin.

"What is it now?"

"Yayyyyy...." Mukitha shouted and pulled out the gift she was expecting.

"He hide it ...stupid fellow always playing tricks on me." she said and looked at it warmly.

Vijji shook her head and muttered under her breath, *"Crazy mad children I have."* She stopped what she was doing and looked at the bowl with a weird expression.

"Mukhi where are the bread pieces I cut to dip in the seasoned butter?" she asked her daughter.

Mukitha came over and made a face that didn't want to announce that her mother had accidently crumpled it into the bowl and made a dough.

"I think that dough was supposed to be your bread sticks mom."

Vijji looked upon in horror and her eyes lifted to watch the chef in the YouTube continue with the procedure, telling the audience to dip the cut thinly sliced bread in the seasoning and place them on a hot tawa. The flame should be medium. Once done the bread sticks were ready.

"What are you going to do mom?" Mukhi asked her.

Vijji suddenly brushed of her shock and said, *"So what if I changed the recipe, I will make bread garlic patties. Vijji special."* she winked at her daughter.

Mukhi always admired her mother's way of treating life. She was one helluva of person who never let anything bother her cheerfulness.

Suddenly *Mukhi* placed a question, *"What's the best Rakhi gift you received from Leela mama (uncle)?"*

Vijji stopped what she was doing and thought about the question placed in front of her. she tasted the bread mixture which was stuck to her fingers. *Mukhi* smiled watching her mother involuntarily action and the gleam in her eyes with the after taste, *"Not bad it tastes yummy."* She said to herself.

"The best Rakhi gift I received from my brother was... after my marriage. I was staying in Indore with daddy and he was working in Ahmedabad. My Rakhi didn't reach my brother in time, the courier was running late.... I was feeling bad and sad too. he had called me to wish me Happy Rakhshabandan in the evening. I felt really guilty. I hesitated to talk to him. He gently coaxed me over the telephone asking what was wrong. I was nearly in tears. I apologized for the Rakhi not yet delivered. And that's when I received my most precious Rakhi gift." Vijji stopped her narration and *Mukhi* felt as if her mother was glowing in a special aura.

"So, what did you receive did your present arrive in time."

"Yes, I had received my Present two days early unlike my late Rakshabandan running late. The words he spoke over the telephone was and is the still the best any sister could receive in this world. My brother said to me EVERDAY IS RAKSHABANDAN, WHEN IT ARRIVES, I WILL CELEBRATE! DATE DOES NOT MATTER!"

CHAPTER VIII

'I will be there...'

She was hesitant to join the group as her mind placed her in a state of question mark.

Radha was a young bride meeting up with her husband *Ananthakrishnan's* colleagues for the first time. *Ananth* was working as a *Research Analyst in BCB (Brooklyn Company of Business)*. He was known for his efficient skills and handling works at minimum space of time. That which saw him grow to the top cadre in a short period. Within a week of *Radha's* marriage with *Ananth* which still left her in a daze and adjust to a new life. She was to play host to her husband's office colleagues whom she would get to interact and get to know them better, she remembered a few faces who had attended their wedding and even got a group photograph clicked with the newlyweds. The marriage album was yet to arrive, so she still had no idea who was who though being introduced.

Ananth walked into the room five minutes later. For after knocking he had waited for her to answer, a response didn't arrive. He understood she was contemplating how to answer him. So, he made a sound as if clearing his throat and pushed the door to the room slowly. Giving her time to face him. As expected, she was standing near the bed dressed in a salwar kameez. Her hair was all over her face and she was pushing it aside from her view. She was looking at her clothes that were laid neatly on the bed and probably deciding.

Radha didn't know how to respond to him or what to call him? She was still scratching her head and talking to herself, *"Okay how about 'Ennenga...or ..."*

When *Ananthkrishnan* walked inside saying, *"Ananth would be fine."*

Radha almost lost her balance on his sudden intervention of her thoughts and telling her how to call him. He took long strides and placed his arm under her back balancing her. With little effort he lifted her made sure she was steady and he went back a few steps giving her space to recover from the unexpected situation.

She felt light, and was taking in a deep breath. She steadied herself catching the bed post and thanked him.

"I am sorry." He apologized to her.

"For what?" Radha asked him catching up on her breath. He looked around and found a water bottle. He was about to get it for her.

"I am fine, that's alright."

He looked at her, *"Sure."*

She gave him a thumbs up sign. Her heart was flustered on his touch and now seeing him in person, sharing space in a room it was kind of a pleasant uneasiness.

Well, it was not that she was seeing him for the first time or sensing his touch. she did steal small glances of him during their marriage and when performing the rituals their fingers and hand did touch momentarily sending sparks in her, she wondered if he felt the same.

Little did she realize he felt the same, and the question she had about him was revolving in his mind too.

He had a demeanor of authority around him. He was slightly on the heavier side, a few inches taller to her. she kind of was off with his oily hair that was combed in a good boy hairstyle. She wanted to tell him about it but again didn't want to force her opinion on him. Right now, her heart melted for the gesture he had done immediately walking in.

"Ananth..." she said slowly.

"Yes." He immediately responded to her. she smiled shyly back at him and haltingly said, *"Nothing I was practicing how to call out your name."*

Ananth nodded his head in agreement, *"Feel free..."* he said and had walked over to the dressing table, searched for a suitable clip and came towards her, he bundled up her hair. It felt soft in his hands and the fragrance of jasmine flowers of last evening lingered on hair.

"Krishna, I can call you right?"

"That's ..." he did not complete his sentence to her. his hands were shaking for his act of clipping her hair.

"If you don't like it, I will call you Ananth." She said quickly. He saw her disappointed reflection in the mirror.

"No...no nothing like that its nice. Krishna...Radhakrishna...I am sorry to have touched your hair without asking permission." He said to her, trying to calm his heart. For when she called him Krishna, he loved it. She smiled and he relaxed.

"Can we cut out on the thank you and sorry?" she said to him.

"It's like we will be doing it forever...as we are now going to stay under the same roof."

He liked her outspoken nature. *"Yeah, sure that would be great."* They then went calm not knowing how to further communicate.

He broke the silence. *"Can I suggest something if you don't mind."*

"Sure, be my guest." She replied.

"But I am your husband." he replied and she was caught surprised.

"Sorry, excuse me?" she asked him.

"Husband...not guest."

"Ahh..." she smiled back at him understanding his joke.

"Sorry about that I couldn't help myself." He replied beaming at her.

"Not bad sir can cut jokes." She told him.

"Sirrr..."

"Give me time to adjust nah I will hound you with your name that you'll wonder why you gave me lenience." She said relaxing to him.

"Waiting for it."

"So, you were saying?" she asked him.

"About this evening's party for my office people, can you ..." he suggested about her dressing and she heard him out. He left after a few minutes. The awkwardness between them was disappearing.

"Krishna..." he called out his name and he liked that she wanted to call him that. Back in his room, he showered and shampooed himself. After drying his wet hair, he tried out various hairstyles, as suggested by her.

Radha when she picked up the saree, he suggested spoke to herself, *"Not bad Krishna, you've an eye for proper dressing. I wonder if he felt bad that I said I didn't like his hairstyle."*

Ananth who was busy with the arrangements and arrival of guests prior her arrival at the lawn where the party was hosted was asked by the guests where was the new bride whom they had come over to congratulate.

He looked at his watch, it clocked 7:00PM. He suddenly felt her presence and looked up, that was when he watched a sheer elegance walk in towards him greeting people comfortably though it was her first time meeting up with them.

She came and stood next to him, with her head slightly bowed. He knew she was still shy facing him. And he felt the same. *Ananth* checked himself for he couldn't stop blushing with her next to him.

She was introduced to the boss and other important personal whom she greeted with a hesitant yet broad smile. The light weight tissue saree was not a hindrance to her faltering step. *Ananth* had asked her to adorn minimal jewelry which she obliged. A single row of American diamonds necklace, with matching studded hangings and a solitaire arm candy vintage stone studded bangle. Her Titan raag watch on her left wrist stood more prominent.

His parent's words uttered a month back still rang in his ears.

"Son if you're not interested in getting married for marriage's sake get us a daughter in law who can be our companion, friend and daughter. You are hardly at home for us to even think we have a son. Thirty-five plus and still unmarried is putting us in a stressful situation." His parents complained.

And when *Radha's* alliance had come over for Ananth his father warned had him, *"I've decided that she is going to our daughter in law and that's final. if you're not interested this time too, I am going to go on a hunger strike eating only snacks and cutting out on rice."*

"Good for your health Appa do that first." Ananth said with a smile while dusted his washed socks on the bench where he was sitting. He bent to pull out black shoes from the shoe rack. He checked if the shine was correct.

His father was miffed, *"I am not going to say no to this proposal, I like this girl and best part is she said OKAY when approached with your details and photograph. Like you mentioned, the girl was asked if she would like to marry you and not forced. She looks friendly and a perfect daughter for our house."*

Ananth was done putting on his shoes, he picked up his business case, checked for his mobile. He then took the photograph from his father's hand and shoved it in his business case. *"Okay fine you can say yes don't need any house visits and tea snacks events direct marriage rituals."* He announced and walked away.

"But he didn't look at her how can he say yes?" his mother voiced her opinion.

"And I forgot please don't do that engagement Hungama too. I am committed to a few projects and deals so I hardly can spare time for all that. Also, Appa don't burden them with dowry, and gifts etc. tell them once the date is fixed, I will book the venue and look into all the arrangements. Don't burden them do you hear me." AnanthKrishnan called out to his parents as he alighted in his car which was waiting for him in the portico, closed the car door, started the engine.

He waited for it warm up and eased it out of the gate. He greeted the watchman who was standing near the open gate, *"How are you Muthusamy today? Did you daughter go to school?"*

The watchman replied, she did and that's when Ananth rolled up the car window glass and switched on the air condition. It was an everyday ritual of his, and *Muthusamy* was always eager to tell him she did. He was indebted to *Ananthkrishnan* for looking after her studies, which was coming from Ananth's pocket, he promised *Muthusamy* he will look after her academics till she settles in a proper career.

"Don't worry our Krishna picked out Radha without seeing means his heart knows he found his soulmate without a glance." Ananthkrishnan's father said in a pleased tone to his wife.

Ananth tried to find the right words to address her, but somehow, he felt his throat go dry. He picked up a champagne flute as it passed by him, offered one to her first and then he helped himself. The drink helped him find courage to talk to his wife. *"If you're okay with it my friends that's my office associates would like to get to know you more. Hope you don't mind I mentioned you are a book enthusiast to them."*

"That's fine." She replied and he felt her voice was soothing like a veena. He took her over to where his friends were and introductions were made. He had to excuse himself as his name was called out from another group.

"Excuse me, I hope you'll be fine? I need to catch with them." He pointed in a direction where *Radha* saw a person signaling to her husband to join them.

"Come on Ananth we can take care of your wife, give us time to get acquainted and pour out your little secrets." One of his colleagues Saraswathi said winking at him.

Light hearted laughter was engaged in the group of six and Ananth left the young bride with them as he strolled over to meet up his other friends.

His heart was left behind with her. wondering if she could manage. And then he recalled their recent conversation and he felt he knew she would not find it difficult. He believed in her.

Radha was hesitant to join the group as her mind was placed in a state of question mark.

Here she was a young bride meeting up with her husband's colleagues, she was asked to mingle as the topic was books, she remembered him asking her what her hobbies were and she showed excitement when she mentioned books.

Then why the dilemma? She scolded herself.

Her thoughts were intervened when she faced an abrupt question immediately after *Ananthkrishnan* departed to join another group.

"Are you a fiction or non-fiction reader?" the questioned directed at her caught her off guard. She glanced at the group who were waiting for her response, and felt the eyes prying at her made her feel queasy.

She called out to *Krishna* the god to put words in her mouth, so she could answer them.

When a glass shattering gave her a diversion. She immediately went about to make sure the mess was tidied and the glass fragments we picked up.

The saved situation gave her a few minutes with the google search on the mobile.

After the mess was cleared and the party atmosphere was back to square one. She walked back confidently addressing the group who were still on the same conversation debating about fiction and non- fiction books.

"Dei I recently purchased two books one was Jay shetty 'Life changing quotes' and another was that motivational speaker Mahatria something...on letters"

"Unposted letter by Mahatria Ra." Radha eased into the group announcing the book name.

"Hey yes...that's the name, did you get to read it.? I picturized you more of a fiction reader." Ananth's colleague Hemanth a tall lanky guy expressed thankfully on being reminded and at the same time hurled an opinion.

Radha took it as a cue and went ahead with a few more words, "I find his writings articulate yet, it has a tone of chatty informal conversation that puts you at ease."

The heads in group nodded in agreement. Radha went ahead with a slight pause, "I am a fiction lover Mr. Hemanth. Love to throw myself into the mind of the author who takes us into the imaginary world of fantasies, crime, thrillers, romance, seriousness and sometimes death. but it never restricted my reading neither my bookshelf which has a well-turned book on science, travel, home improvement, religion, art and music not forgetting the motivational books we just spoke about."

She shared a beaming smile with the group members, *Saraswati* grinned hearing Radha's words. She was enjoying the look on her colleague Hemanth's face.

"At last mister know all getting small gyaan that too from ladies." Saraswati rooted for Radha silently in her mind, *"Bravo gal for letting them know the difference and that these non-fiction books are also picked up and read by some fiction readers."* She raised her glass in salute.

Radha blinked her eyes in acknowledgment at *Saraswati* whilst continuing. *"As far as my knowledge goes, I think non- fiction doesn't restrict only to self help and biographies, history! It's a literature based in fact and broadcast category of literature. So, channeling me to being a fictional reader I think is too fast deriving at an opinion."*

"Of course, not at all. I didn't mean to categorize you." Hemanth said agreeing with her. and the group went ahead discussing more topics on books and travel. *Ananth* smiled watching his wife having a lively conversation and getting comfortable with the guests.

Fifteen years to this memory *Radha* thought as she closed her wedding album. She looked across the living room, *Krishna* was immersed watching Wimbledon.

She uttered the words in her mind, *"Can I say I love you to you Krishna? will you be able to hear my silent love."*

He suddenly turned and looked at her and smiled as if reciprocating he loved her more than she did.

It sent butterflies flying in her stomach. Till date she still fell in love with this guy every second. He was not the type to bring home flowers or surprise gifts, shower her with praises.

"I will be there for you no matter what." A promise he gave her on their wedding day and till date he never faltered from it. Just like the day when she was in a dilemma wondering how to differentiate between fiction and non-fiction readers. He had deliberately tripped a glass and passed on his mobile phone that had the google search app answer her question.

Some stories don't need a constant love moment, being there for each other speaks volumes!

CHAPTER IX

An Attire to remember?

"What has a dress got to with molesting me? Are you not going to say anything to him?"

Sheila watched the annoyed faces staring back at her from the breakfast table. Her entire family had gathered for *Nadira's* marriage at her paternal grandfather's place. Nadira was Hema aunty, her father *Jatin's* little sister's daughter. It was the first marriage of their generation being celebrated and Sheila's grandfather insisted it take place in their ancestral house. *Nadira* was the first grandchild of the family.

It was blast meeting up with cousins from all over the world.

Sheila and her family had come over to *Rajasthan* all the way from *California*.

The first week was a perfect holiday to remember. The cousins gang hit it out with trekking, pool party, dress rehearsals, dance practicing for the D-day and loads of other fun activities. Two days before the horrid event *Sheila* had encountered, *Nadira* the bride to be had tagged *Sheila* to the temple. Just the two of them. It was the time of dusk by the time they reached the temple. They had a divine darshan and after that both the girls relaxed sitting down near the temple outward steps which faced the westside. Both watched the sunset after a spiritual moment with their family deity. The temple was situated on a small hill top. It had a ghat road for the vehicles to enter, but the girls parked the car in the parking lot below and preferred to take the 350 steps to the temple.

Nadira shared a piece of prasad. It was made with dry fruits and jaggery.

"Life throws you unexpected twists when you are enjoying it right shells?" Nadira said with a note of seriousness.

"Hmm." Was all *Sheila* said to her.

Nadira called her shells, in short for *Sheila* and Sheila in return called her *Nad the mad*. The cousins hardly spoke for a while, they give in to watching the sun set.

"Feeling a weight on me, that's making me depressed shells."

"You all happies right with the groom and marriage stuff Nad?" *Sheila* had asked her.

"Absolutely." *Nadira* replied defensively.

"I could not have asked for a better being to be my better half, Manoj is a perfect partner."

Sheila laughed out. *"Then what's with all this philosophy talk madam, chal it doesn't suit you. we are all into chill party gal. stop behaving as if it's an arranged marriage."*

Nadira and *Manoj* had been seeing each other for the past five years and shared a live in relationship for two years in Delhi where they worked. After a lot of hue and cry. With family sittings, including zoom calls, facetime and discussions. Their marriage was approved.

Sheila pointed her litter finger at *Nadira* and said, *"Damn oops sorry we are in a temple, I should have recorded your expression. Is that your standard answer to the family."* And she imitated *Nadira*. *"I couldn't have asked for a better partner. Cut the crap gal."*

Nadira smiled sheepishly.

Sheila suddenly cut to the point, "okay madam what's bothering you, out with it." She caught her cousin's hand and asked her suddenly.

Sheila could feel the hesitation on *Nadira's* hands. Gently she pulled them back, and tried to divert by adjusting her chunni.

"You can tell me idiot what's bothering you?" *Sheila* coaxed her cousin. *"I've been noticing from day one I arrived you were not so your usual self. I thought it's because you're getting married and you were nervous about it. But during our outings you seemed aloof. What's eating that little brain of yours. You know right we have no secrets."*

Sheila caught *Nadira's* hand and pressed it gently. She then patted it reassuringly trying to relax *Nadira* and make her talk.

"Shells, just in case like think okay, not that it happened I am like you know telling you in case if I happened. No, its not I, I mean if one of my friends confided in me that she witnessed something which is not correct but the person is a family member what do we do? Do we tell on the person or keep quiet and ..." Nadira's voice trailed off.

Sheila knew better and didn't question her further about who that friend was. She sensed *Nadira* had come across something and it was eating her up. She weighed the subject and her cousin's anxiety.

"Nads, if it's bothering you a lot..."

"Not me shells, my friend." Nadira correctedherpromptly.

"Yeah, sorry my bad. I mean if it's bothering your friend and talking about it helps ask her to. There is no such thing as a stranger and family member. When something one witnessed is wrong. You should voice out."

Before *Nadira* could reply, their cousin's gang caught up with them and a surprise visit by the groom Manoj ended the topic there.

After two days, *Sheila* was blasting the family for taking the side of a perverted person≥

"Damn ..." Sheila cursed.

"Nads, are you worried that your marriage will be stopped? Do you want me to shut up like the elders of our family are suggesting?" Sheila questioned her cousin.

"Don't bring her into this now, Sheila. For god's sake Jatin tell your daughter this is not the right time for all this drama." Aparna *aunty* spoke. She was *Jatin* that is *Sheila's* father's elder sister.

She hit a vase that was placed on a pedestal near the French window where she was standing. It shattered with a bit of sound but, the gasps and comments that were voiced seemed louder and more fatal.

"Look at her acting up as if the devil is residing in her." it was *Aparna* aunty again. she was a spinster and everyone took her advice for she was the elder after her father who was mostly considered a retired person.

"Come to your sense girl, we have people walking in and out of our house and shut up with all these accusations. Ghar mein shaadi hai ladki. I hope you understand." She lectured her.

"And I always knew something like this will happen with all that little clothes and sleeveless you wear and walk around the house. see I can see your bra strap peeping out from your thin see-through shirt or whatever you call that thing you're wearing." Aparna aunty voiced her opinion with a disgust on her face.

"Sheila please bacha leave it dad will look into it." Mahima Sheila's mother tried to comfort her.

Sheila was enraged at her family's reaction. She was screaming her head out that her maternal uncle tried to rape her last night at his daughter's sangeet function. And here her family was trying to point the accusing finger at her improper dressing and not him.

"Sheila kindly stop the drama now, we all saw you enjoying a couple of drinks beta. Now don't throw accusations, its Nadira's wedding and we don't need any situations that can make her feel discomfort." Sheila's aunt *Manya* spoke trying to put sense into her. *Manya* was *Jatin's* younger brother dev's wife. He too nodded his head agreeing to his wife.

"Sheila beta sometimes we need to turn the other side. He is not an outsider. And that thing you're saying well no one can for you see there is no witness and he is the son-in-law ..." Sheila lifted her hand to slap her uncle in a fit of rage and controlled her anger.

"What the hell..." she shouted back.

"Do I look like a fool to throw statements that are not true? Do you think I knew this incident was going to happen so I should be ready with a camera and film it? Are you guys out of your senses. This guy is a bloody and instead of supporting me you're asking me to shut up are you even my family?" She pointed her finger at her uncle.

Her cheek smarted with pain; it was her father.

"Enough...can't you see grandfather is sitting right there and you are creating a scene. Think of Nadira. Keep your thoughts to yourself and we can discuss about it later."

"Hell with later papa. What nonsense is this. Why should we bury secrets and act normal. I am your daughter papa; I am telling you without feeling embarrassed that this bloody animal touched me. cannot you hear me. are you deaf." She shouted and fell on the floor dejected.

"Stop it Sheila go back to your room right now and pack up. I want you out of this house." Jatin Sheila's father announced.

She lifted her gaze to watch her uncle's reaction. He stood there with a smirk on his face, he lifted his eyebrows at her state as if telling her see no one can do anything about it. He shrugged his shoulders and spoke to the gathered family.

"I am at fault I admit, yes I am guilty." He announced.

"See I told you; he is and he admits it."

He walked up to Sheila and placed his hand as if comforting on her shoulder. She literally threw it aside, "Don't you dare touch me you filthy bloody abusing molester."

"Sheila." Her father called out to her. *"Let him talk."* Her father walked up to *Sheila* and stood in-between her uncle and her.

"See all of you saw She was wearing a low neckline blouse and short skirt. She had too many drinks and was almost in an unconscious state. So, I helped her to her room. Once inside she puked, I couldn't leave her like that. Bacha hai. She is like my daughter. And everyone was busy with sangeet. So, I thought let me clean up and keep her tidy. Is that wrong do tell me? I looked at her like my daughter and she was intoxicated probably she felt I was one of her boyfriends and you can guess..."

"Seriously that's your explanation." Sheila looked at him unbelievingly.

"You ass...you undressed me completely and your zipper was down. I was not completely drunk I threw you off me, when you kept smothering me with your horrible kisses pervert." She suddenly pounced on him, if her father would've not come in between, she would've wrenched his eyes out.

"He was also drunk so..." was the justification given by the elders.

"It needs to be hushed up, because family sticks together." Was the judgement passed out.

Sheila looked at her parents, *"Dad seriously are you in for it. Mom, I cannot believe it ma. What's going on. Are you for serious guys. I hate this family thing business. Come on family sticks together for trouble times and lifting up one and other. Will no one speak up for me. is this what a family stands for."*

The cook serving breakfast answered on behalf of *Sheila, "I wear a saree and still he touched me."* The room went silent though they were ten people in it.

She stood shivering catching the serving tray, "He threatened to throw my husband in jail who works in his mine and also put a robbery case on me if I won't listen to him. Sheila beti is correct. He touches badly."

"Hey you servant, shut up your mouth." Sheila's uncle shouted at her.

"I caught her stealing jewelry and her husband is one big crook. She begged me to reconsider. Bad lady she was the one who offered her body. I told her to behave and kept quiet because they have small children. If I throw them out of work, how will they survive. They won't have food."

he glared at her and spat, "I should've thrown you out of the house long back."

None dared to speak, and furthermore the situation went chaotic when a tiny voice, gasps spoke up. It was the gardener's ten-year-old daughter who stood by the door watching the tamasha.

"He gives me chocolates every time he visits, I don't want it, because it pains. I don't like chocolate anymore."

"I saw him...touching her." it was Nadira who spoke.

There was loud slap and everyone came to senses after the stunning revelation. Nadira's father *Ashok* was lying on the floor and Sheila's grandfather was standing beside him. He gave one look at both his son's.

Sheila's father *Jatin* and his younger brother Dev thrashed him.

"The reason I kept quiet was because, I didn't want to hurt my father. You dare to touch my daughter. I didn't keep quiet because I believed you. I kept quiet because of Nadira and my sister. I was planning to kill you tonight. You touch my daughter is it." Jatin shouted and thrashed him.

Sheila stood watching. Her tears wouldn't stop but she felt a sense of relief. The truth had come out.

The accused uncle's wife Savitha placed a call to the police station immediately, hearing the atrocities, her hands shook as she dialed and her head hung in shame for, she was a pervert's wife!

Savitha looked at the body in the mortuary and hardly spoke a word. The memory attached with the dead person suddenly evaporated. Both her brothers lead her out of the hospital and she got into the car heading back to her home, her father's home to be precise. Previously she used to stay next door to her father's house. after the incident, *Ashok* was handed over to the police. She vacated her house and came over to stay with her father and elder sister.

She converted her house into an orphanage and rescue house for the needy it was an idea *Sheila* had given her. She found solace running it and felt it was cleanse for the sins committed by her husband. Though she had no knowledge and such atrocities were being done right under her nose, she felt she was a part of it.

Her mobile rang bringing her out of her memories, she answered it. *Nadira* her daughter was video calling her from her in laws place, she didn't talk about the mortuary visit but both her brothers *Jatin* and *Dev* along with her were happy to converse with a pregnant Nadira who was inquiring when will they be coming to take her home for delivery?

CHAPTER X

Open your eyes!

What a weird name Prabhu sir you came up with for your recent podcast?" the Television interviewer whose name was *Sharma* appreciated and cleverly threw a question as to why it was named as such.

Prabhu looked at his hands and adjusted his watch. He was seated in a couch into which he relaxed himself and grinned, while rubbed his nose with his right thumb at the interviewer. Prabhu carried a down to earth personality, but his dressing style always drew attention. His famous *Calvin Klein Shirts* and *Hugo boss glasses* could be called a trademark style of his. The baldness gave him a serious look, but in reality, he was an extrovert. People put him on the high pedestal for he was a *connoisseur*. At sixty he carried a vibe of a teenager.

"Are not titles supposed to be different to attract the audience like your program?" he replied gently returning the ball into *Sharma's* court.

"Of course, of course." Sharma replied in humor. Sharma turned his attention at the camera which was rolling and spoke with confidence, he knew the BGM added later would highlight his words. This was a recording that was to be telecasted the next day in the 7 PM slot of their channel.

*"Okay then let's start with the formalities you've already heard the casual remark of our guest tonight and let me introduce you once again audience of **'Talk the Talk with Sharma'** I am your humble host Sharma and our guest today is none other than the Hulchul Podcaster Mr. Prabhuratna dev."*

Sharma now swirled the chair to face *Prabhu* and shared a handshake before started with his first question.

"So Mr.Prabhuratna Dev..."

"Prabhu would be fine. Every time I hear you mention my full name it's like I am back to school and on roll call. I stop myself from standing up obediently and saying present sir."

Bothshared *a* laughand *Sharma* resumed, *"Sure, Prabhurat excuse me ...Prabhu Sir. So, as I've introduced you to my audience as a podcaster and yes many have an idea what a podcast is, still it would be a help if you could let the audience understand and know what a podcast is? But before that how come you've chosen this media? At the age of sixty plus you've given the retirement card to former job and now creating a buzz with your podcast, how did you come across this and what made you want to be a podcaster? What made you opt for it? Did you know prior the pulse of reaching out to listeners? How did you manage to secure a large following? The topics..."*

Prabhu coughed loudly. *Sharma* stopped.

He picked up the bottled water placed on the table and offered it to *Prabhu.*

Prabhu refused and grinned at *Sharma, "I am good thank you, by the way Is this a rapid-fire interview that throws questions and hardly waits for the answers I've been invited too? I am sorry I didn't prepare for it. Or am I supposed to hear all the questions at a go and then go about it?"*

Sharma drew his hands up in a giving up manner and said timing out, *"Okay I think I went overboard with questions. We get to hear your voice every time the podcast plays. I was in that momentum and felt if the questions could be finished at the earliest possible, I can relax and hear you talk without any interruptions."*

Sharma was quick witted, after all he had been in the television industry for last ten years and this show had celebrated a year and half, **'Talk the talk with Sharma'** it was quite popular from the time it was aired. *Sharma* knew the audience plus and invited the most trending celebrities the people were familiar with and felt a connection.

Prabhu smiled and took it light hearted.

"So can I?" he requested *Sharma* in a jovial manner if he could go ahead with it.

Sharma had already picked up his coffee mug and looked towards the camera and announced.

"Tonight, I am an audience like you'll. Prabhu Sir will come up with a brief description of what a podcast is and tonight we are but concentrating on his recent Audio which took the world, I am not exaggerating but yes, the Audio had become viral. So, the show begins ladies and gentleman don't miss out even on a single word. The show does have a repeat telecast on Saturday night at 10 PM, but watching it excitedly the first time its aired has its essence which cannot be found in a repeated telecast. Ladies and gentleman I present you the trending Podcaster our very own man from our city Prabhuratna Dev.

Prabhu smiled and jovially said, "Present sir." Lifting his right hand.

"Attendance taken." Sharma reciprocated with a grin. "Let's begin the show."

Podcast is nothing but an audio series you get to hear for a couple of minutes preferably in your free time. Its available in digital format apps that can be downloaded for free mostly through internet and a description follows that helps you choose, like how shall I tell you. something you get see in a bookstore visit. You get to choose what audio interests you and play it. So, a podcast is mostly a single person or a host interviewing another like a talk show, which is scripted carefully. You could say a discussion or content on a particular topic or current events. A few podcasters walk back memories with movies, songs, books, people and events. Some journal trips and places that can be visited, spiritual talks, motivation the list goes on. A proper soundtrack is carefully added to enhance the listeners relaxation and feel comfortable.

"Okay wonderful." Sharma comments and asks him, "So why?"

"I am sorry I didn't get that?"

"I mean why a podcast?" Sharma cleared his throat, "How did you channel your way to it, social media video journals are many. So why a Podcast?"

"Hmm, how shall I frame this for you..." Prabhu adjusted himself in his seat, picked up the water bottle gulped a bit and replaced the cap.

"Okay, let's see during the covid times, I felt the loneliness creep in. not that I didn't have my family around. But missed the usual walks and discussion with my friends or a gathering of people. Mobiles we there, video calls and other things kept one busy, but the urge to talk one's mind. Well, I missed that. that's when I happened to chance upon this audio talk. It seemed interesting. I googled about it and followed the necessary instructions. I ordered the necessary equipment, set up my base in my study and then I drew a blank."

"Excuse me." Sharma asked surprisingly.

"Yes, I drew a blank not knowing what to talk, as soon I as went near the mic I felt the urge mic testing, mic testing 1,2,3 check."

Sharma interrupted, "So that's how the famous tagline of your podcast churned out, through a blooper is it."

"You can safely bet on that." Prabhu replied jokingly.

"I felt a consternation. I had no clue how to start or what topic to present. When I was a young chap, I wanted to be a journalist, then a radio jockey. I secretly had stashed my journal books in my cupboard. I took them out and flipped the pages. I happened penned my thoughts on everyday musings and people I met. How life was treating them. So, I summarized short Auto fiction stories. Real life incidents with names and places changed. Stories that needed ears to feel their minds. 'SILENT STORIES' started picking up momentum with my batch and then the family obliged, I literally had to threaten my children and grandchildren to promote me, lots of under the table dealings also happened with them." Prabhu laughed when he stated that last line.

"I don't think so it was necessary, I am an ardent fan of your podcast and listen in detail. I like the way you draw a line of narration only to five minutes." Shamra appreciated Prabhu.

"Thank you that is considerate of you."

"My favourite was School Galatta that was featured in your SILENT STORIES, you got us all involved in the story. It didn't feel like a remembrance of good olden days but as if it was happening again in the present. The words connected not only to the yesteryears or middle aged but the current students to checked themselves with it. You have an art of storytelling must say. Not everyone can hold an audience attention. Not one episode of yours felt okay let me hear it later. Once it was played, I am sure like me people would've been mesmerized hearing you talk."

Prabhu nodded his head on receiving the compliment and remained silent.

"So, the recent podcast of yours..." Sharma let the sentence trail. He waited for a minute or so. The question he asked hung like ice between them.

He was about to place the question again when Prabhu took a deep breath, exhaled and started to answer.

"Open your eyes... hmm that podcast drained me. I spoke about it after a six-month gap. Not that I didn't want to talk about it, the hurt somehow felt personal. It was unexpected and took me through a whirlwind of emotions. Facing a trauma is one thing and trying to heal is a completely different chapter. After a certain conversation I got to hear, it dawned on me that wounds though heal can leave a nasty unseen scar. Though a person is rescued form the emotional trauma the healing can never be complete. It's like a physical bleeding and affects every aspect of the person's life. Traumatic experience changes not only the fundamental style of living, but give them a nasty psychological outlook view."

Prabhu paused.

Sharma contemplated and then put forth his request gently, "*I know you have spoken about it in the podcast but can you give us a briefing on* '**Open your eyes...**'".

The interview went on with Prabhu surfacing a few more details and Sharma wrapped up with his witty one liner and once again flashed the details of Prabhu's Podcast. He informed his audience where the links would be available for them listeners who had not had the opportunity to hear the recent one and also get to learn a lot more about life and different out look through Prabhu's voice.

The goodbyes were exchanged and other details were discussed. *Prabhu* excusedhimself for he was wanted elsewhere.

After getting into his car, he drove directly to the beach and stopped at secluded place. It was late night. He placed his phone on airplane mode and watched the waves Splashing against the rocks. He was filled with anger. he had spoken about many taboo topics recently but then realized when the person you speak to is your near and dear and you had no idea, they had faced a traumatic situation. Somehow the hurt is deeper. The stain doesn't leave you, and life seems horrid at a certain point of view.

"Open your eyes.... God dammit." He shouted.

His fingers rolled into a tight fist and he hit the car bonnet. A dent was seen which was not relevant now. Many incidents they had spoken about countless times in groups, functions and even condemned them. And to think one of their own was subjected to it in front of their bloody noses which went ignored, no not ignored. they had no idea though everyone's eyes were open.

He shouted out till his lungs burned. And his eyes starred to tear. *"What the hell...."*

He shouted again. *"Dammit I went to a studio to talk about this topic. I cannot believe it."*

He felt exactly the waves throwing themselves against the rocks. It was not hm who faced it, but a known person. but hearing the voice narrating though it happened years back. The pain was still raw and like the waves it seemed they were not hurt when thcy touch the rocks roughly, yet merely watching them make one feel the hit. And now he was in the same position. he could feel the trauma and mental state of the victim.

Prabhu visited the memory he had spoken in his podcast. Two weeks back it was released and immediately, raged like fire and had become a hot topic.

"I feel like a corpse today. A corpse that has something to tell you. a living corpse." Prabhu laughed sarcastically.

"We all live in a world of delusion don't we, poking our bloody noses in other people's businesses and voicing out judgements on their

problems and issues. Advising them how to lead their lives. I remember this small story I think I read somewhere or must have seen in a social media post. It's about a lady who keeps looking out of her window every day. The husband gets curious and asks her why she spends time watching the neighbors. She complains to him about their neighbor being lazy and I wonder why her husband doesn't even tell her that their windows are dirty. The husband after hearing his wife out picks up a dusting cloth and rubs against their window, which clears of a dust.

That's one damn reality bite.

Not only that lady but all of us are living in the same agenda. No idea how our household is progressing but, stick our nose and criticize our neighbor.

I will tell you why I narrated the previous bit because it is a direct hit about what I am going to talk about now.

A few months back I happened to receive a call late night, from a known number. I wondered if it was distress call? Late nights always send a shiver down my spine for maybe 9 out of 10 times I heard a sad news. I think most of you'll would agree on it.

The caller took time to exchange pleasantries and I reciprocated the same. Not to exaggerate but my previous Podcast did garner attention, which was heard by the person. I received feedback appreciating my story telling style. What else does a Podcaster need than a good word. That's when a request was placed.

Can a story I tell also be Podcasted through you? I replied I could give it a try to make it heard to a minimum audience at least. And the conversation proceeded. It took a long time from my side to digest what was heard. The known caller had hung up with a verbal note from myside that maybe one day I shall be able to go ahead with the narration. I need time to talk about what I heard.

Trust me, it was hard and still **IS** because I am conjuring words yet unable to cut down to the conversation that shook me up. Every day we wake up to atrocities we get to read in print media, shared through social platforms. We discuss, feel the rage utter a few verbal abuses, accuse the person who had committed the crime and get back to work. Hands dusted for we've done our good deed by expression, thought or perhaps a few good Samaritans help monetarily. Let me ask you a question, is our household safe from an evil glance? Do we even have an inkling of what's going at home, yet we generate vigor to talk about topics related to others and pass on opinions.

Imagine a well-known family, that holds a name in the community. No -no that's not how I want to start this narration. Let me try my hand at it once more, hmm.

"I was raped not once or twice but multiple times." The voice said almost in a whisper.

The shock that shook me and made me forget to breath for a minute or so and then I had to cough as the air filled my lungs. Damn the world, damn them, damn right. What the hell. I took a few deep breathes and tried to come back to my senses, it was the line that followed immediately that threw me into a stupor.

(The following content will be narrated as a first person, that is in the voice of the person who had approached me.)

"Raped by my own brother and when I called out for help, I was used like a past time toy by my other cousin and..."

The person choked on the words.

"It's okay if it's difficult we can do it another time." I suggested.

"No..." the persons agony, anger and anguish that was bottled for years was seen in her response of No.

The person cleared her throat and continued.

"I was weak in studies and ..." a pausc again. this timc I kncw not to interfere. I was not in a position to let the receiver think I was on line and listening. I stayed quiet and let my loud breathing assure her I was there.

"Okay well..." a deep breath was taken on the other side and continued with the memory that was hurting her badly.

"As you know my father had passed on when I was a child. And ours was a joint family which resided in a mansion of house.

"I being the youngest in the family. People around always thought I was a spoilt brat and being treated to luxury. My elder brother was already an adolescent studying in a hostel. We had an age gap of

nine years. He was a holiday visitor at home. My elder sister, born after him was a matured and well-behaved girl. She was apple of the family's eye as she never had a hair out of place and was studious. The youngest that I was had trouble with my books, and everything the world offered in a simple manner. I loved to keep myself entertained with the glitz and glamour of parties that were a normal at home every other day. Watching people dressed in jewelry, those fancy sarees and party wears, house bustling with decorators. Cars lining up to drop or pick up celebrities. My eyes sparkled and the child's eagerness to catch on details to take the next day at school had become habitual.

We children were always under the scanner of the housekeeper or cook or any help who hand a bit of free time to keep an eye on us. My report card had red ink numbers that was a bother to my mother. Yet she had no time to check upon me for devotion towards family and other things. As you know I had lost my father when I was a baby. My elder brother who had come over for his vacation from hostel comforted my mother he would take care of my studies. During the initial days it was a stick that smarted me every time I made a mistake. He would sit on a chair opposite to me and I would be cross legged on the floor. The beatings decreased and I felt that I was improving. The chair had moved forward and his hand was always on my shoulder. Sometimes the hand would slip and linger a few seconds more with a slight press on my teenage growth. I kept my mouth shut scolding myself for he was my elder and in my father's place. He is teaching me and, in that progress, when his concentration was intense, he probably, unconsciously touched me. But this continued for a while. The chair was discarded and he placed himself next to me. his moves became bolder. I hated it. But I was thrashed and then subjected to this inappropriate torture. Reason I was failing in my studies. I tried to complain to my mother saying I had discomfort with his presence. But my mother dismissed me asking me to behave and take advantage of him when he is around for, he was only a monthly visitor. They trusted him blindly and he made sure they were blind to his brutality towards me.

How could I tell her he was taking advantage of me? he was my own brother. Not a friend or cousin but own flesh and blood. I then convinced my school teacher to take up tuition classes for me and the bargain went well. The Rakshasa that was the name I had given him arrived after a month. He called me to his room, and I managed to escape by citing I was home tutored. The Rascal came up with another plan and convinced my mother and teacher that when he was around, he would take care of me. I was back in his clutches and my body was always sour with pain which was not noticed by any family member though the house was filled with people. None even bothered when I missed my meals. I could hardly join my friends for play. My legs bore blackish blue marks which made me walk slow. People dismissed my fatigue reasoning with my illness. For I frequently had seizures.

This torture continued for a while, and once it so happened the door of the room where I was kept a prisoner in the name of studies was not locked properly and a cousin of mine walked in and saw the Rakshasa using me. His gasp I felt was going to be my survival. Before the devil could turn to see who or what the disturbance was, and noticed the door slightly ajar. My cousin by then had hid himself. The devil then went and locked the door.

After the devil had left the cousin consoled me and patted me, I was exhausted and rested on my cousin for support I cried my heart out. And in the name of sympathy and consoling by the cousin whom I didn't have strength to fight as my body was already in pain and I was used again mercilessly.

After that I swallowed sleeping pills, the irony of my situation. None arrived when I was used but came to my rescue immediately when I attempted suicide. I tried to run away from school but I was searched for, and coming from a reputed family I was instantly recognized and taken home. I jumped from the terrace but a shamiyana tent was put up for an event that broke my fall and gave me bruises. I cut myself with a razor, since my hand shivered on self-inflicting wound it was not fatal. All these attempts were dismissed citing my illness and being poor in studies.

My brother, cousin and his friends everyone walked into the house with a mask of goodness and used me like a plate. Yes, a plate because our house was known for its grand lunches and dinners. Parties with delicious delicacies served on precious plates. Precious what a way to term myself because I am white skinned and the mirror, I looked into not for admiring myself but reflected back a beauty that I hated and the opposite sex greedily shared amongst themselves. How bad can it go when you cry in the four-wheeler and the driver also uses you. was I willingly giving myself up to the hunters. This thought too ate me up. I happened to see a documentary of a lion chasing a deer, how much every it evaded from his clutches in the end it fell prey. Either to this majestic animal or the jackals who feasted on the left-over carcass. In the end you are a waste piece of flesh. I felt the same.

When a prospective groom had come over to our house, I felt happy I had a chance to escape. But the groom after looking at me felt I was underaged. I somehow managed to secure his address and get an audience with him. I pleaded him to marry me, then divorce me so I can get away from the devil's clutches. He too walked over to me and placed his hand on my shoulder. I cringed but his touch was fatherly. The marriage proposal was accepted and after five years of nightmare by my own brother and other sex offenders I saw daylight.

My husband encouraged me to pursue my education, took me to doctor sessions, therapies and until I fell in love with him, he never touched me like a man. Now I am a grandmother but the wound is still raw. I felt a connection when I heard your podcast that lifted a finger against the wrongs of the society and how you spoke about the common people and their stories. I felt my story too should be heard and I trust that none other than you can make the world sit up and hear.

The house maybe a mansion, wealth maybe in multiples but a child always needs a parent's attention. Family is important when you are in a large one. But so are children. When a child is constantly falling sick ask them what's wrong?

When a child stop eating find out why?

When a child goes silent don't think it's in obedience but coax the reason out?

When child attempts suicide awake yourself to a red light blinking on your face and hear the distress signal that they are in danger.

Live for the society, only after you raise your child in a safe environment. Let the child know you are there and also will listen attentively to their talk. That's when the child will come out with their feelings. Lunches, dinners, parties, events, occasions, gatherings, visiting's all these can take a backseat when a child comes and clutches your hand in fear.

When your own family members and relatives abuse you whom will you turn towards and ask for help? I hated my life then, after getting married felt I was living on borrowed time and feelings. I could not come to terms that I was loved because, I somehow felt maybe it's a sympathetic love towards me. that's a worst one can face. no matter the assurances, the heart still fears and doubts.

This topic is cringe I know but I don't want to take my memory to the grave. I want this memory though bad revisited and spoken about. In that manner, at least one will look back and notice what is happening with their child.

I trust you'll manage and let my story be heard.

Take your time, I will not change my mind and take you to task once the story comes out.

I will wait for it.

The call disconnected.

It took me six months to come to terms with what I heard and frame it into a story.

"As a podcaster I could feel the emotions and trauma as the victim because to emote the feelings of the particular person one has to understand the circumstances again and again until the right words fall in place and reach out to the audience. The writer in me had to frame a script first and that needs a pulse to connect so that the audience can feelthewordsspoken and experience the trauma mentally to understand why it was spoken about.

My agenda here is not to throw a bruise the wound of an old scar.

To at least stop one wound turning into a nightmare scar.

Signing off for now

Prabhuratna Dev until I cross path with another common man/ woman who needs their suppressed voice to be heard."

Prabhu stood standing for a long time watching the waves. He had no idea when he compromised with himself and drove back home.

When he was in the middle of his interview, he had received a text from her. which he checked after he was done for his phone was in silent mode.

"Thank you for taking my story to the people. I feel peaceful at last."

There was another message which was received five minutes later in the family group.

She was no more.

Prabhu said to himself as he maneuvered the car towards the highway, *"She had fought her demons enough let her be at peace."*

CHAPTER XI

Watching Stories

Manohar was hardly sipping his chai, he sat idle on the wooden bench placed near the tea stall, watching the people walk by.

He looked lost to others.

A glance at him, people would sum up that, *"Poor guy something bad is eating him up."*

Yet none stopped to enquire. Why would they, people are so busy in this mechanical world of social media that phone messaging played a major communication. Not a live conversation. Manohar maybe a chanced speculative story for the inquisitive eyes who noticed his regular ritual at the tea stall. Arrival at 5:30 AM on the dot and stilling aloof till 8 AM.

He never indulged in conversations with anyone, always if noticed was seen sitting with a chai glass in his hand with a faraway stare.

This tea stall which he visited on regular basis was two streets away from his rented apartment.

He was witness to the morning walker's regime, the newspaper enthusiasts or should they be called the undercover government advisers who were never satisfied and seen debating issues and churning out ideas that even the ruling party had no inkling about. Some were experts in the international government bill summary too.

The chaiwallah, how can we leave this sports person behind without a word or two mentioning his skills. The angry man irritated that the badminton racket didn't swing in the right angle he had opinionated in the prior games. Cricket players were not sparred too.

The next group, a few health-conscious ladies gathering, always judging an ornament that it must be artificial but the person was showing it off as gold. Or that dress must have been bought dead cheap but passed on as a branded clothing.

Now, the education conversationalists, the anxiety fathers discussing children's education that they have selected.

Suddenly this regular buzzed environment was interrupted with a person's gasp, *"The weekly short story by 'WATCHING STORIES.' is out, did anyone read it?"*

"I just did." One person said and continued, *"Very realistic."*

"I agree."

"I wish this anonymous Author, writes daily."

"Me too same feeling. The short stories sometimes feel like it's happened, how shall I state it? As if we experienced it and this person was lurking in the shadows and writing about it. Remember the previous one it was a Deja vu feeling when I read it. That incident mentioned was similar to what happened to me."

"Exactly and that December issue..." another spectator interrupted, *"It was too good the storyline."*

"Yeah, it was but that incident felt like I was reading my mine."

"Don't tell me, yeah now that you mentioned, you said the same on that too."

"I second that."

"I wait to read them, gives a break from the serious monotonous articles we read every day in print and social media too." a middle-aged man came up to join the group, he rested his hand on his friend's shoulder.

"Rajan four cutting chai's." he called out wiping the sweat of his forehead with his handkerchief. He carefully folded the soiled handkerchief and tucked it into his trouser pocket. The wife will definitely throw a fit when she gets to pull it out and the air around her will fill with his you know that hmmm sweat fragrance.

"So, what did our anonymous writer today?" he asked after his handkerchief ordeal.

"You'll choke on the chai if I tell you." the group member who held the newspaper spoke with a mischievous look in his eyes.

"Stop the drama or hand over the paper, I will read it." The handkerchief man said. He tapped on his friend's shoulder and asked him to move a bit so he came also sit amongst them on the

bench.

"Okay fine I will brief you." the man who got to read the story first said in an authoritative tone. Why would he not for he had the groups spotlight fall on him.

"Arre Venu remember that special celebration of your in laws coming over to your house and giving their blessings after 6 months of your elopement?"

"What about it? as if none of you have love stories, I became a hero because I took a decision to marry and standby my true love." The man boasted.

"Okay what about it, was it mentioned in the story? Now hurry up and tell me."

"Ha okay, okay now hero. We all know your chase, hiding and marriage part. Listen to this now. That incident of when your parents were coming over to see your wife for the first time after marriage...and that chicken curry episode where your wife cooked special dishes and asked you...."

"Oh that, Lakshmi was busy from morning trying her best to perfect the recipes and when I reminded her to change into a sari, she left me in charge of the almost done curry." Venu said chuckling to himself.

"Ha that one, and the ingenious thing you that day?" the man who held the newspaper questioned him.

Manohar who was an invisible spectator, shook his head and smiled. He got up from the bench. Stretched a bit, paid for his chai. he walked past the group who didn't even bother to look up at him.

"Excuse me..." Someone called out to him.

Manohar halted in his steps. He turned to face him. *"Your Aadhaar card."* The person handed it over.

"Thank you." Manohar reciprocated after receiving it back.

"When you paid it fell from your back pocket and this too." he was informed as a matter of fact.

Manohar paused when he saw his work identity card in his hand.

"Be careful with your things." The middle-aged man said in an advising tone.

"Yeah, sure thanks." Manohar said smiling.

"New around here?" he was further probed.

"Oh, you work in the newspaper is it." He saw the group attention turn towards him.

Manohar just nodded his head in affirmation. The man flipped the identity card and handed it over without any interest. *Manohar* received his cards and started back to his apartment. That's when he heard them talk about him.

"Who is he?"

"I don't know."

"You were saying newspaper, did he write the story or what?"

"Arre no man, I saw his identity card and it had a newspaper name on it. That's why I asked. Didn't notice his designation."

"Anyways he doesn't seem like a writer."

"Who knows." Someonesaid with a doubt.

"Where does he stay?"

Rajan the chaiwallah replied, *"He stays at Sharma's. he is a PG there."*

"What job?"

"Don't know he comes sits drinks chai, goes back. I then see him in the evenings riding a bike. Doesn't talk much. No friends."

Manohar took out his mobile and dialed a number, *"Relocating."* that's all he said.

He listened for a few seconds and kept nodding his head to the person whom he called.

"Yep, I know it's been two months but I find this area self-proclaimed detectives. Imight get busted. Anyways I already have ample sheets of their conversations, need to find new ones. "

He grinned for the reply he received and cut the call, *"Yeah who is not a detective in this world. All neighbors are interested in the others life than the stories happening in their houses. Am I not one too?"*

He turned to look at his favorite group chit chatters. And started to narrate the story written in the newspaper.

"When his wife asked him to add lime to the finished curry and throw it out. The husband obediently squeezed lime and switched of the burner. Lifted the hot curry and threw the contents. That's when

Venu hears his Lakshmi's gasp. He realized his mistake and hits his head. the wife broke down. He assured he will set things right. The wife brother calls at the moment and listens to the disaster that had happened. He suggests a take away. His siter's husband shakes his head negatively saying his parents disapprove outside food. The call which was spoken with the speaker on, on both sides gets disconnected. The doorbell rings. The husband fears it's his parents and the daughter in law feels she will never be accepted.

Venu the husband opens the door and his wife Lakshmi's mother walks in with a steaming hot chicken curry. without a word its placed majestically beside all the previously prepared dishes. The Husbands parents walk in. after a few uncomfortable moments of introduction, everyone relax over lunch. Lakshmi looks at the almost empty chicken curry bowl and thanks it silently for uniting the families."

Manohar stops at this and thinks, "I should have written she thanked the lemons!"

As he turns towards his street, he starts whistling a popular tune. His mind running thoughts in tune with his happy tune, **"Anotherarea, another tea spot and ears get to hear while the eyes watch new stories."**

Everyone is a storyteller, who lives in the network of stories they experience. Because, when everyone has a story to tell, whether its whispered or yelled. The creative eyes get to watch them, the attentive hand enjoys a travel of ink filled pages. Stories can sometimes be inspired by a line spoken by someone somewhere with a sudden burst of energy. An incident that was recalled. A sigh that made one feel weak. But that doesn't mean it lacks originality.

To sentence it into a simpler tone, they are like presents wrapped artistically and gifted with an intention that the receiver can feel that its special and theirs alone.

'Memories'

Everyone has memories that's a fact, which cannot be denied, the heads nodding in unison is the basic truth of agreement while reading these lines. And however, the memories are remembered with love. The story that happened and is in continuity with the play button on in the mindset makes them unique love stories.

Stories are inspiring, while some have wounds and some have feelings. But some make you take a deep breath and wipe a tear with a sunshine smile!

Well, my dear readers when you glance into the world of memory it's because the love, bond, feelings, expressions for that particular incident to happen was triggered with love for a particular person. A love that plays hide and seek with its relationships.

I managed to chronicle such stories to bring them forth to you.

Why?

Because they have a fairytale touch to them.

When a question is raised, do these fairy tales exist? Well, witnessing these stories I believe they do! For memories remind us nothing lasts forever, like a Giant wheel what goes up has to come down. Instead of counting the days as they pass by, we should but allow the days to count. For time is precious. We can be happy today, sad tomorrow.

Let the tale of mixed emotions gather around us and make a million feelings, thousand thoughts with stories from memories.

Until next time with more stories from me to you, this is PRASANTHI POTHINA signing off!